A Snow Garden

and Other Stories

www.**transworldbooks**.co.uk

Also by Rachel Joyce:

The Unlikely Pilgrimage of Harold Fry
Perfect
The Love Song of Miss Queenie Hennessy

For more information on Rachel Joyce and her books,
see her website at www.rachel-joyce.co.uk

A Snow Garden

and Other Stories

Rachel Joyce

Doubleday

LONDON • TORONTO • SYDNEY • AUCKLAND • JOHANNESBURG

TRANSWORLD PUBLISHERS
61–63 Uxbridge Road, London W5 5SA
www.transworldbooks.co.uk

Transworld is part of the Penguin Random House group of companies
whose addresses can be found at global.penguinrandomhouse.com

First published in Great Britain in 2015 by Doubleday
an imprint of Transworld Publishers

An early version of 'A Faraway Smell of Lemon' was first published as a digital
short story by Transworld Publishers in 2013. 'The Boxing Day Ball' first
appeared in the *Observer* in December 2014.

A CIP catalogue record for this book
is available from the British Library.

ISBN 9780857523532

Typeset in 11½/15pt Berkeley Old Style by Falcon Oast Graphic Art Ltd.
Printed and bound by Clays Ltd, Bungay, Suffolk.

Penguin Random House is committed to a sustainable
future for our business, our readers and our planet. This book
is made from Forest Stewardship Council® certified paper.

1 3 5 7 9 10 8 6 4 2

For Kezia May, because you always liked a short story.

A society grows great when old men plant trees
whose shade they know they will never sit in.

Greek proverb

Contents

Foreword

There is a joke I like about an actress playing the nurse in *Romeo and Juliet*. Someone asks her what the play is about.

Now the nurse is a nice part for an older woman. She gets a few laughs. She's seen a thing or two and she voices the things the audience longs to hear – so we like her. But let's face it, she only has a few scenes and she's not Juliet. She probably gets one costume and the chances are it's a tabard, along with some sort of uncomfortable and slightly insane-looking headdress, a thing with horns and a veil.

Anyway, the actress thinks very carefully about how best to summarize the plot of *Romeo and Juliet* and then she says, 'Well, it's all about this *nurse* . . .'

We are at the centre of our own stories. And sometimes it is hard to believe that we are not at the centre of other people's. But I love the fact that you can brush past a person with your own story, your own life, so big in your mind and at the same time be a simple passer-by in someone else's. A walk-on part.

Like most things, this book did not end up as the thing it began as. It was meant to be three stories. (It's seven.) They were not meant to be linked. (They are.) It was meant to be a comparatively small, quick project. (It wasn't.)

When I write – whether it's fiction or plays, and even when I adapt other people's novels for radio – I make lots of cuts. Words go. Descriptions go. Passages. Chapters. And sometimes, yes, entire characters. As much as I may like those words or descriptions or characters, if they are holding up the story and getting in its way, they end up being deleted. And this is why I have the idea of my caravan (where I write) being stuffed with people I have cut from my writing. Binny, for example, who is the main character in the first story of this collection, was no more than an extra in an early draft of my second novel *Perfect*, but she was too big for the book and threatened to over-topple it. Very reluctantly I cut her. Henry, who 'lives' in the title story, was originally a rehearsal for a character in the new novel I'm working on called *The Music Shop*. Alan and Alice, the married couple in the second story, were once in an afternoon play and had ambitions for bigger things – a film maybe, but that never happened. Then there is a story about a young woman called Maureen going to a local dance, and while I kept her in *The Unlikely Pilgrimage of Harold Fry*, I couldn't keep the story of how

10

her life changed that night. Sometimes I picture all these 'cut' characters stuffed in my caravan, making a nuisance of themselves, and the racket is quite something. So I loved the idea that I could clean them out, as it were, by giving each of them a short story of their own.

(I still have a batch of curates that I had to delete when I was dramatizing Charlotte Brontë's *Shirley* for BBC Radio 4. They spend entire days in my caravan gossiping and drinking tea, and I have no idea what I am going to do with them. If you would like to adopt them, they are available.)

Stories are important. We need them. It is through telling and hearing stories that we make sense of the world. Like dreams, they come to us when we are quiet and they tell us something or remind us of something that we need to hear. They say to us, *No, you're not alone. Because that thing you feel, I feel it too.* And sometimes they ask us to think again.

The appeal for me of a *short* story is that it is like a dream *and* it is like life; a curtain sweeps open briefly and at a key point in someone's history you are allowed to sit so close you can see the creases, the dimples and the freckles of their skin, and then – whoosh – the curtain closes and they have gone.

A Faraway Smell of Lemon

It is half past nine and Oliver will be eating porridge in his Asterix bowl. At the age of thirty-three he has no regular habits but these – the porridge and the bowl – and he is faithful to both.

'Sod him,' Binny snorts, striding into the morning traffic. Pavements jostle with Christmas shoppers. The city streets are dull beneath the December cloud and when the sun breaks through it is white as the moon. A giant billboard shows an image of a pretty young woman in a 1960s-style red coat looking up at snow. Shop windows twinkle with lights and tinsel decorations and illuminated messages wishing good will to all men. 'Sod him,' Binny repeats. No, no, no. She will not cry.

Now that she has dropped off the children at school for their last day of term, Binny has five hours to fix Christmas. As a girl, she was brought up by her parents to love it – the parties, the food, the presents, the decorations – but this year she has done nothing. She hasn't bought a tree (they don't need one). She hasn't ordered a turkey (they'll never finish it). She hasn't posted cards to any of the people who have sent her cards and neither has she bought presents or tubes of metallic gift-wrap. This morning, Coco pinned two large woollen slipper socks above the mantelpiece for herself and Luke. ('Just so we don't forget on the day,' she said.) If only the machine that is Christmas would come and go without Binny.

She spots one of the school mothers jogging towards her like an aerobic fairy. Binny freezes, searching for an escape, but she is not the sort of person who can easily hide.

Tall and broad, Binny towers over other people, even if she stoops. And she does, she does it all the time, she is always stooping and slouching and digging her hands into her pockets in an attempt to make herself lesser. She is dressed, as always, in something black and shapeless she found tangled on the end of her foot this morning as she staggered towards the bathroom.

The jogging mother does not look like the sort of person who wears screwed-up versions of what she had on the day before. She wears a candy-pink jogging suit with a fur trim. She is something to do with the school PTA, but Binny can't for the life of her remember what, because Binny never opens the emails and she never attends the functions. If she stands very still – if she pretends that she is not here – maybe the woman will bounce along and not notice her.

'Binny!' the happy jogging suit calls. 'Hiya!' She shouts something that might be about the Nativity play but a double-decker bus roars past. The advertisement with the young woman in her red coat seems to be all over that too.

The Nativity play will be performed this afternoon. Only it is not a Nativity play, as the children keep reminding her, it is a *Winter Celebration*. It was just last night, as he climbed into bed, that Luke revealed he was playing the part of Larry the Lizard. 'But there was no lizard in the Nativity,' said Binny. 'This *isn't* the Nativity,' sighed Luke. And Coco added, 'Our headmistress says the Nativity is not multicultural and also there are no parts for girls. Except Mary.' 'But there's no lizard in *any* religious festival,' said Binny. 'Larry the Lizard is Buzz Lightyear's friend,' said Luke. 'What?' said Binny. 'Buzz Lightyear has nothing to do with Christmas! You never see him in *any* Christmas scene!' And Coco said, 'Well, Larry is very significant. He sings the solo from *Frozen*. Also, I am the Ghost of Christmas Past.' When Binny complained that it was no good, she couldn't run up a lizard costume at the drop of a hat, no one could, and actually the Ghost of

Christmas Past was in another bloody story altogether, by Charles Dickens, as it happens, Coco and Luke had exchanged a small but solemn nod. 'It's all right, Mum,' said Coco gently. 'Meera's mum made our costumes. Luke has a blue tail with spikes and everything. I am going to have a lamp and a fur hat and also a sari.' Coco seemed more than happy about that. She didn't mind at all.

Binny did mind. She minded very much. She wanted to be a good mother, but here were all these others, being not just good mothers but super-mothers. Did Charles Dickens realize, all those years ago, as he wrote about snow scenes and Christmas spirits, not to mention roast goose and country-dancing, what he had gone and started? Was it not hard enough trying to bring up two children and work part-time, without having to stage an annual Christmas pageant as well?

The jogging suit is so close there is no hope of escape. There will have to be a conversation and the jogging suit will ask if Binny is all sorted for Christmas, and How is Oliver? and Isn't he nice? and Binny will want to scream. No, she is not all sorted. Her heart has been broken. Snapped in two. What is the point of Christmas? What she really wants is to deal the blow as brutally as it was landed on her, and to watch someone else reel and give in to the tide of grief that Binny herself will not allow.

Instead she slams her hand to her head to suggest that she has just remembered something crucial – a last-minute piece of shopping, such as the turkey, for instance – and bounds towards the nearest shop. The fresh cuts on her hands sting like tiny prickles as she pushes open the door.

It is as if Binny has stepped through a curtain and discovered an alternative universe. It's been here for ever, this shop, but she's never bothered to come inside, just as she's never bothered with the boutique next door that sells party frocks and wedding dresses. For a moment she stands very still in this strange, new place where the dust swirls like glitter. The silence is unearthly. There are shelves and shelves of cleaning products. They come in jars, canisters and bottles, some plastic, some glass, all arranged at regular intervals and in order of size. There are displays of brushes, cloths, scourers, dusters – both the feathered and the yellow variety. There are boxes of gloves – heavy-duty, latex, nitrile, polythene – as well as Kentucky mops, squeegees, litter-pickers and brooms. Binny had no idea that cleaning could be so complicated. Right beside the till stands a small plastic angel, the only clue as to the time of year. She has a halo and a crinkly white dress and two pointed tinsel wings. There is a smell Binny can't put a name to, but it makes her think of lemon peel. Clearly there is nothing here for a woman like herself.

She is about to retreat when a female voice chimes through the silence, 'Can I help?'

Binny squints in the direction of the voice and sees a slight young woman gliding towards her. Her skin is a flawless ivory and her deep-brown eyes are like seeds, as if she is studying Binny from inside a porcelain mask. She must be in her early twenties. She wears a crisp uniform that suggests a dentist's but surely can't be, and her black hair is caught in a polished ponytail. The young woman stands with her hands at her side and her crepe-soled shoes not quite touching, as if physical untidiness would be offensive.

At the age of ten, Coco is the only one in Binny's house who understands tidiness. Luke does not understand it (because, he says, he's only eight) and Binny doesn't understand it either, although she is forty-seven. The daughter of a naval officer and a girdled socialite who had people 'who did', Binny has made a point of embracing chaos. Her home is bound in a thicket of ivy. The small rooms are so packed with her parents' Victorian furniture ('Junk,' Oliver calls – no, *called* – it) that most of them have been reduced to passageways. Surfaces are felted with dust and piled high with old magazines and newspapers and tax returns and letters she has never bothered to answer. The carpet is thick with dust balls the size of candyfloss, screwed-up clothes on their way to the washing machine and nuggets of Lego, and in the middle of the sitting room there is a dead shrub that the children have been using for a Christmas tree. They have decorated it with cut-out paper snowmen and pigeon feathers and brightly coloured sweet wrappers.

'Don't you sell stuff for someone like me?' asks Binny. 'Paracetamol or coffee or something?'

The young woman is curt. Not exactly rude, but she isn't friendly. 'This is a family business. We've never sold anything but cleaning products. We supply mainly to hotels. And also corporate catering.'

Binny examines the bottles that gleam from the top shelves like coloured eyes. *Keep out of the reach of small children. Phosphoric acid. Benzyl salicylate. If swallowed DO NOT INDUCE VOMITING.* 'Is this stuff legal?'

'We don't sell a product if we can't guarantee it will work. We are not like those supermarkets where the bleach you buy is water. For instance, some bathroom cleaners are specifically for shower tiles and some react badly with the grouting. You have to take these things into account.'

'I suppose you do. I don't have a shower. At least, I do,

21

but it has no door. And the water doesn't shower. It sort of dumps on you.'

'That's a shame,' the young woman says.

'It is,' agrees Binny.

'You should get it fixed.'

'I won't, though.'

The shower is one of the things Oliver has spent the last three years promising to mend. The Hoover is another. Oliver is messy-haired, easy-going, slightly fuzzy at the edges, always wearing his T-shirt inside out and socks that don't match. He can spend minutes untangling loose change from his trouser pocket for anyone who happens to hold out a hand and ask for it. The rest of the time he is so busy gazing at the sky that Binny has long suspected he will one day flap his arms and soar upwards.

It never used to matter that Oliver was a good twelve years younger than Binny and had no regular income because he was an actor who couldn't get what he called 'proper acting work', only voice-overs or the odd commercial. It never used to matter that he always left the keys to the van in the driver's door and forgot about things like replacing toilet rolls. It never used to matter that he might go to fix the shower and notice his reflection in the bathroom mirror and drift straight back to the kitchen to ask Binny if she had some concealer because he was afraid he might have a spot coming.

But their loving had become commonplace. They had stopped noticing the otherness of one another and now that otherness was no longer a source of wonder but instead an irritation. Binny cussed every time she walked into his guitar at the foot of the bed. Or, 'Why must you always use the moisturizer?' she'd complain. 'I didn't think you'd mind, Bin.' 'I *mind* because you never replace it and you always leave the lid off.' 'Well, I won't use it then,' he would shrug. 'But if it were mine, I'd just share.' He would wander upstairs to play his guitar, leaving her even grouchier because now she felt not only disgruntled but also less generous than him. Playing his guitar was what Oliver did when he was sad. His songs offered an escape to a land where girls had long hair and wept over Irish seas. They were beautiful in their way, even if they were childlike.

However, the shop woman is still talking. She is still on cleaning fluids. 'Of course, you can't use some materials on plastic. Or carpets. Even lino you must be careful with. You have to match the product to the problem.'

This is anathema to Binny. Surely there is clean or not clean? And in her house there is only the latter. She tries to find a new point of contact. 'Where I live, there's a smell. I don't know what it's of. It's been there years.'

'Drains?' Despite herself, the assistant looks very interested.

'No. It's more like . . . old things. The past. You get it differently in different parts of the house. For instance, upstairs, just outside the loo, I can definitely smell my ex-husband's aftershave and we divorced six years ago. Or other times I'll get this overwhelming scent of my mother's jasmine soap. Then there was a friend I had once when I was a girl. She was a few years younger than me but we did everything together, and then she got married after university and we lost touch. I still get a whiff of her rose-oil perfume once in a while. Do you think the memory of a smell can hang about in a room? Would you have anything for that?'

'For the memory of a smell?' The assistant frowns.

'No, of course you don't. Basically the house is covered in shit.'

'Is this connected to the smell?'

'*Metaphorical* shit.' Binny laughs. She regrets it instantly. It sounds like the sort of thing her ex-husband used to say. It sounds as if she thinks she's clever.

Her intelligence is not something she likes to flaunt. It's the same with her body, and also her feelings. When her mother died a few years ago, hot on the heels of her father, Binny refused to cry. 'You must let go,' her friends urged.

'You must grieve.' She wouldn't, though. To cry was to acknowledge that something was well and truly over. Besides, given the size of her, it felt dangerous. She might swamp the world. Instead she stopped seeing her friends.

Binny tells the young woman, 'Our Hoover broke. My partner was going to fix it. I don't think he actually *knows* how to fix things. He just wishes he was the sort of person who could mend Hoovers, so he says the kind of things they would say.'

'Does it suck?'

'I beg your pardon?'

'Your Hoover?' The young woman gives a small intake of breath to indicate what she means. It sounds like the tidiest hiccup. 'Maybe all you need is a new bag.'

'If only *life* were that simple,' says Binny. 'What do you suggest for the heart?'

The young woman is looking confused again.

'Joke,' Binny reassures her.

'Yes,' says the young woman. But she is not laughing.

The real joke is that Binny believed things were beginning to look up for her and Oliver. About two weeks ago he'd bought her a Christmas present. She knew because he'd left it on the driving seat of the van (she discovered it when she was hunting for the keys). It was a bottle of her

25

favourite perfume in a special gift box. They'd made love that night and again the next. It wasn't abandoned, like at the very beginning, when the need for one another was like eating. But it was familiar: faces breathing smiles in the dark, skin on skin, the honey warmth of him. Oliver's kisses were beautiful things; his mouth opened over hers, as if he was giving a part of himself that was unavailable at other times. Silently he had moved within her until deep inside she opened like a flower.

A few days later he'd limped barefoot into the kitchen, dancing the weight from his left foot as if the sole was shot with invisible nails. 'Ooh,' he'd sighed like one of the children, waiting to be noticed. 'Ooh, ooh, ooh.'

'Morning, Ols.'

'Where's Coco? She said she'd find me a plaster.'

'She's at school, hon. It's quarter past nine. Why do you want a plaster?'

'Ooh, ooh,' he'd repeated, hobbling to a chair. 'I've got a verruca, Bin. Coco took a look. It hurts. It hurts a hell of a lot, actually. I don't know why you're smiling. It's not exactly very nice.'

She'd said not to be a weed. Let her have a look, she'd said.

And when she did, she saw his toenails. Silvery blue, they shimmered like mermaid scales, with little black hairs sprouting below the nails. 'Hey, Ols, what's with the nail varnish?'

'Oh,' he said, appearing to remember something insignificant. 'Oh yes, Sally did those.'

'Sally?' she said.

And then it all came out.

Binny and Oliver sat at opposite sides of the kitchen table and spoke quietly. There was no anger. They even smiled. They forgot about the verruca. Holding her hand in his, studying her fingers as if he'd lost something in them, Oliver explained how he'd met Sally when he did the breakfast-cereal commercial a few months ago. She was in advertising. Hated it, of course.

'Of course.' Binny found herself siding with Sally as if she were a friend. And this was strange when she had lost touch with so many real ones. 'But you're not in love with her or anything?' It was a joke. She was expecting him to say no.

Instead he said, 'This is so confusing for me.'

She felt a ping of alarm.

'Yes,' she said; well, it was getting quite confusing for her too.

'Sally is really excited about what she believes. Not like all those mothers in the playground first thing in the morning. They look as if they can't *remember* what they believe.'

'At that particular moment they've got their hands full. They're amazed they've got their kids to school, for one thing. And that they're dressed, for another.' She laughed to show how fun she was.

Oliver continued talking earnestly to her fingernails. 'Sally's got so many opinions. She collects ideas like . . . I don't know . . . like other women buy shoes. She keeps me thinking. I know this sounds mad, but you'd really like her, Bin.'

Binny felt an impulse to shout and sat on it. 'I don't suppose that's important,' she said. 'Also, not *all* women buy shoes.'

'I know I'm an arse.'

'No, you're not,' she said.

Oliver sighed. He sank his head to the table, as if he couldn't bear the weight of it. Binny glimpsed beneath his T-shirt the secret smooth skin of his shoulders and the sprinkling of freckles. His back would be golden again by the summer and the freckles would be washed away. She longed to slip her hand down there, to touch the warm softness of him. She thought of lying naked at his side and then her heart took a plunge. She realized with a terrible, blank and absolute clarity that it was over.

'What's up, Bin?' said Oliver. 'You've gone a funny colour.'

'I'm just trying to understand.'

She would never touch his bare skin again. From this moment onwards they must behave like two people who only knew one another in clothes. Her breath was snatched clean out of her. She felt hollowed.

'I wanted to say something to you before,' he said. 'I *should* have said something. I just couldn't bring myself to do it, Bin. Oh, I feel really shit.'

'No, no, you mustn't,' she said, groping for the companionship of his fingers. But he dipped his hand between his knees and her arm was left shipwrecked on the table.

Oliver told her that Sally loved all the words to his songs. (I love them too, thought Binny; I just didn't tell you.) Sally said he was a gifted musician, as well as an actor. 'It's not just the sex,' he added. They had only done it six times. Twice after the commercial, twice in the van—

'Not *my* van?' gasped Binny. The words shot out. She never normally referred to things as her own.

—and twice at her parents' place.

'Her *parents*'?'

'She's moved out. She had to. Now there's going to be a baby.'

Binny slumped as if she'd been walloped in the spine. Sex? Parents? Baby? There was not enough room in her lungs for the words and the breath and the emotions that were beginning to swell there in an amorphous gloop.

Oliver flexed his silvery-blue toes. His eyes melted. 'I'm sorry, Bin. I've got to do the decent thing. I mean, I'm only realizing this as I say it. I kind of hoped the problem would go away on its own. But it's because of you, Bin.'

'What's because of me, hon?'

'You're such a good person. Now I'm telling you, I'm sort of seeing it through your eyes. And I'm seeing I've got to stick by her. She's petrified. She needs me.'

Binny gazed at him, and tried to speak, but couldn't. All she knew was that nothing made sense, as if someone had cut a space out of time and had failed to tell her.

Then, 'No!' she roared. She thumped the table so hard that the piled-up breakfast bowls jumped and chattered. 'What about Coco? And Luke? What about *me*?'

'I know, Bin, you're right. And I'm heartbroken that I've lost you. But what would *you* do?'

So his mind was made up. *I've lost you.* Already Binny and her children existed in the past tense. She swallowed, but the lump in her throat stuck like a stone. 'Well you'd better go,' she said.

'Shall I have my porridge first?' he said.

It took barely an hour for Oliver to snip the shape of himself out of Binny's life and paste it into someone else's.

She piled his bag and his guitar into the van, along with his Asterix bowl, and she gave him a lift to Sally's new council flat. He buzzed at the door and waited, rubbing his thick hair with his knuckles until a girl shape appeared at a high-up window. Sally looked tiny all the way up there, like a little bird framed with coloured fairy lights.

'Bye, Ols.' Binny lifted her hand to wave. It looked more like a 'halt' sign.

Oliver turned and his face was dark and tangled up. 'Oh, I left you some perfume,' he said. 'In the bathroom.'

And that was the end of it. So straightforward. So simple.

Except, of course, it wasn't. Binny found that what had seemed to be an acceptable level of pain that morning became searingly unacceptable once he was gone. She had been seduced by his kind, milky voice and the regular flow of his words into behaving as if what he had told her was bearable. But it was not. She felt the lack of Oliver's guitar when she failed to crash into it in the mornings, just as she felt the lack of him when her moisturizing cream remained in the same place, with the lid on. No one made porridge at half past nine and no one left the saucepan on the worktop, or a sticky rim of honey on the table. She stared at the places where his things had once been and all she could feel was that they should still be there. His absence became a presence and she thought of nothing else. She binned the perfume.

The children brought home paper angels and pictures like stained-glass windows that fluttered from the mantelpiece every time she banged the front door. They sang from their bedroom about Good King Winsylass and We Three Kings of Ori 'n' Tar. Luke said he would like a go-kart for Christmas. Coco said she wanted to give a goat for charity. Only she wanted to keep the goat in their back garden. 'But the poor people who need the goat live in Africa,' said Binny. 'That is racist, actually,' said Coco. 'There are some very poor people who live down the road.' Overwhelmed, Binny bought nothing.

And every evening it was the same question: 'Where's Oliver?'

'He's gone away for a while, Coco.'

'I'll wait up.'

'I wouldn't.'

The little girl pursed her neat mouth. 'I think I will, though.'

So Binny did not buy a Christmas tree or get out the box of decorations from the loft or fill the kitchen with mince pies and jars of pickle. It was all so futile. But she'd catch her daughter at the window, waiting for the person Binny knew she couldn't make appear, and she was overcome. It was worse than hoping for Father Christmas. She'd kick the washing. Slam the doors. Rail at the mass of winter sky, flat and grey as a Tupperware lid. But nothing, nothing eased her fury.

Last night she'd finally given in. When the children were in bed, she had watched a programme showing the hundred funniest moments in television – she'd laughed at not one of them – and drunk a bottle of red wine. After that she had phoned Oliver. Why shouldn't she? She didn't even know what she was planning to say. And when he didn't answer, as she knew all along he wouldn't, she tried again and then again. Now that she had started this thing that she hadn't wanted to do in the first place, she couldn't stop. She tried maybe a hundred times in all. And every time he failed to answer she felt increasingly diminished and increasingly betrayed.

'I am not here,' his voicemail message told her, over and over. 'I am not here. I am not here.'

Knowing Oliver, he'd probably lost his phone. It was most likely in a bar somewhere or slipped between the cushions of a sofa. And then a new thought had come to her; a real thorn. What if the mobile was not lost? What if he and Sally were lying in bed, clinging to one another like beautiful weeds, *choosing* not to answer? In Binny's mind the couple sent her a closed-off smile.

How *dare* Oliver find peace when she had none? How dare he replace her and be so easily, so stupidly happy? Did her love mean *nothing*? She hurled the empty wine bottle at the kitchen wall. To her surprise, it did not break. It bounced off the fridge into a pile of dirty washing and returned dog-like to her feet. And because the bottle would not smash, she grabbed her mother's best Royal Doulton plates from the dresser and shot them at the floor. One by one.

They broke. Oh yes. They splintered into a thousand blue ceramic pins. And then she bent over the pieces, the only thing she had left of her parents, and her face yawned into one gigantic noiseless scream.

'Mum,' Coco said in the morning, on discovering the wreckage, 'I think we had better buy breakfast in the garage shop today.' She closed the kitchen door as if it were better Binny did not see.

It was too much. All too much. But *I will not cry*. Emotion washed up and over Binny, and still she would not surrender to it. While the children were finding their song sheets, she swept the splinters of china into her hands and squeezed until they spiked her skin. Then she shoved her feet into trainers – Luke's actually – and slammed her front door so hard that the pane of glass tinkled.

'Bollocks,' she told it.

The children skipped ahead, counting Christmas trees in windows. *'Away in a manger,'* sang Coco, *'no crib for a bed.'* And Luke sang, *'The little Lord Jesus laid down his sweet legs.'*

But now it is past ten o'clock on a mild and damp morning and Oliver will have finished his porridge. Her children are rehearsing a Winter Celebration about Larry the Lizard and Buzz Lightyear while Binny stands alone in the middle of a shop that stocks nothing but cleaning products. How could this place be less appropriate? Deep inside her, something is stretching and expanding and she has to clench her jaw to keep a grip.

'So can I help you?' asks the young woman. This could be the third time she's asked the question, but if it is she doesn't raise her voice or speak with any sign of impatience.

'I probably need a dustpan and brush, to start with. For my kitchen floor.'

'Are we talking wood or marble?'

'We're talking crappy lino. Does it really make a difference?'

'It affects the brush.'

The assistant fetches a ladder and reaches for a chrome dustpan. She pulls out several brushes and examines them, running her fingers through the bristles. 'This is the one,' she says. When she returns from her ladder she is smiling. *How easy it is to be you*, thinks Binny.

'You don't like cleaning, do you?' says the young woman.

'I find it hard to waste my time on something that is just going to get dirty again. If it's any consolation, it's the same with the ironing.'

'Domestic chores can be therapeutic.'

'So can red wine,' says Binny.

To her surprise, the young woman laughs. 'It's small things that make a difference. Something that you know you can do if you take the time. It's important to have those things. If I was a painter I would paint, but I am not a painter and so I don't. Cleaning is what I like. I take a piece of silver. I apply the polish with a duster and I wipe it all over. Then I take a fresh duster – nice and clean – and I rub carefully. Ages, I can do that. Tears will be running down my face, and I'll keep polishing till it's over. It always works.'

The young woman looks directly at Binny. Tears running down her smooth, pale face? It's hard to believe.

Nevertheless there is something in her eyes, something shiny, like Coco when she has hidden a coin behind her back. Suddenly she doesn't look so young any more and neither does she look tidy in that hygienic sort of way. She asks, 'What happened to your hands?'

'Oh.' Binny steals a guilty glance at the tiny cuts. 'I had an accident.' She expects the young woman to move away, but she doesn't; if anything the young woman looks even more carefully, as if she recognizes hands like these.

'Maybe you would like me to show you? How to polish?'

'Me?'

'Why not?'

Without waiting for an answer, the young woman walks to the cash till, bends to retrieve something from beneath the counter and produces a shoebox. She sets it on the counter beside the Christmas angel with her tinsel wings. For a moment she gazes at the box with her hands suspended in the space above it, as if it contains hallowed treasure. Then she takes off the cardboard lid and places it beside the box.

Inside there is one folded duster and another duster wrapped around something small, along with a pot of cream. She removes the pot, the folded duster and the one in a bundle. She places them just-so on the counter. She unscrews the lid from the pot and shows Binny the white cream inside. Binny gets the lemon smell again. Slowly and carefully, the young woman unwraps the bundle and reveals a small, silver christening cup.

'Life is hard sometimes,' she says, lifting the cup from its duster wrapping. 'And that's a fact.' She balances it between the tips of her thumb and forefinger and lifts it to the light. Transfixed, she stares at the cup, and so does Binny. It is about the size of Coco's fist and the handle is the slimmest crescent moon, so delicate an adult finger will not fit inside. Below the rim there is an illegible inscription in a swirling font. At its centre the cup bears a gleaming reflection of both Binny's face and the young woman's.

With her right hand, the young woman rolls the duster into a cigar shape and dips the end into the cream. She rubs it all over the cup's surface until it is smeared white. Clearly she's done this many times before. Her tongue tip rests on the corner of her mouth as, without looking, she flaps open her second duster and begins to polish. It is beautiful the way she does it, so carefully and in such tiny perfect circles.

'Five years ago I lost my baby,' says the young woman. 'He was stillborn. He was so little I had to bury him in doll's clothes. They were pink and I wanted them to be blue so I cried. But when he was dressed I didn't care about the pink any more.'

'I am so sorry,' murmurs Binny.

'It was Christmas. Everyone was happy. I felt like I didn't belong.' She continues to wipe and wipe.

Binny has a feeling like a bubble in her stomach and she doesn't know why but it rises up, up, up. Without warning, something warm slants down the side of Binny's nose towards her mouth. It tastes of salt. She knocks it with the heel of her hand, but here come more. Tears. It's the grace of this young woman that unpicks her, the way she keeps wiping. With her tears come images from the past, images of people Binny has loved and lost. Her parents, Oliver, boyfriends, her ex-husband, old friends, Alice with her rose-oil smell, even people she passes every day on the street and does not know. So many lives somehow tangled with hers, gone now, or going. So much love, so much energy, and for what? It all seems to smell of lemon.

Fresh tears well from Binny's eyes and swamp her cheeks, her chin, her hair. It is so big, this feeling, it is hard to believe she is alone with it. Are there moments when those people we remember are plunged simultaneously and without warning into the same ocean of memory? Is it possible that Oliver, for instance, is at this very moment recalling the curve of Binny's thigh and picking up his guitar and singing from a high-up window while the Christmas lights blink over a housing estate? She cries and stops and wipes her eyes, and then she cries some more.

'Would you like a tissue?' The young woman magics one from her pocket.

Binny blows her nose with a honk. 'This is not something I do. I can take anything. I mean, look at me. I'm a rock. I *never* cry.'

'You wouldn't be human if you didn't. Do you want a go?'

'I'm sorry?'

'You can if you like.' The young woman offers the tiny silver cup and the yellow duster. 'Try not to touch the surface. Then you won't get finger marks and smudges. You want to do it properly.'

Binny wipes her hands carefully on her coat. She receives the small, cold christening cup like a gift in the cradle of her palm, her whole body tensed. It touches the cuts on her hands, but it is so light they do not hurt. If anything, it soothes them.

'That's it,' says the young woman. She tucks the duster into Binny's right hand and guides it, as if Binny is blind, to the pot of cream. 'Gently now,' she says.

Binny scoops up a tiny spot of polish. She dabs it over

the cup. She takes the second cloth, the polishing one, and she rubs with tiny circular movements all over, up and down, left and right, just as the young woman showed her. She thinks of nothing except the silver cup, how it was covered in white and how, as she polishes, the silver returns. She balances it between her fingertips, holding only the base and the rim. She mustn't smudge.

'You have to accept it, don't you?' says the young woman. 'He's gone.'

Binny continues to wipe the duster in the smallest concentric circles. Briefly she closes her eyes and breathes in the lemon smell.

A memory comes back. It is so clear, she sees it. It is herself as a girl. It is Bronnley soap on a rope. Of course. Sherbet-yellow and shaped like a small, dimpled balloon. She is pulling it out of her stocking, tugging off the paper, and everything, everything smells of lemon, even the satsuma and walnut hidden at the bottom. The whole of Christmas will smell of it. 'What do you have, darling?' Her parents laugh as if they have never seen such a thing as soap on a rope. It is that simple. And every year it is the same. The soap, the smell.

When she opens her eyes, the young woman is watching. Binny holds the cup very still.

'I am sorry you lost your baby,' she says.

'It's nice to talk about him. People don't want to see me upset so they don't mention him.'

'Did he have a name?'

'I called him Gabriel.' She points to the engraved writing. 'Because of the time of year.'

'You must hate Christmas.'

'No. I like it.'

Binny pokes a corner of the first duster into the pot of cream, just as the young woman showed her, and rubs again. She takes the second duster and begins to polish.

'My partner left me,' she says at last.

Her words echo in the silence. The young woman nods. And because she does not reply, because she does not fight Binny's words, because she does not soften or dilute them with a sentence of her own, they fall for the first time. They land. Binny feels their weight, her loss, but the world does not stop or shudder. Yes, she is still standing. She is still breathing.

And so Binny dares to think of those other people she has lost. No matter how much she rails, some of them are gone for ever. The young woman is right. Some things we can have only briefly. So why, then, do we behave as if everything we have connected with, everything we have blessed with our loving, should be ours for keeps? It is enough to have tiptoed to that space which is beyond the skin, beyond our nerve endings, and to have glimpsed that which beforehand we could not even imagine.

'I don't promise cleaning is the answer to everything.' Saying this makes the young woman laugh. 'You could try something else. Chop wood. Or make soup. Sometimes you just need to do something ordinary. Something you don't need to think about, you just do. And there are times, too, when it's nice to show someone what you've done. When it's nice to hear them say, *Yes, that's very good. I like that.*'

How has she become so wise, this unassuming young woman?

So Binny will make a start on the kitchen. She will get a tree for the children to hang with their homemade decorations. She will buy cards and write messages. It's still a few days until Christmas; it's not too late. She will find little gifts, rubbish really – soap on a roap, a satsuma, to wrap and stuff in those woollen slipper socks hanging on the mantelpiece. She will join the ritual of acknowledging what she has loved, either with an email or a sparkling snow scene. She will remind the people who are left that they mean something to her, even after all these years, even after all this separation. This is what her Christmas will be.

'Gently, gently,' smiles the young woman. 'Look, you've missed that tiny bit beneath the handle.'

Time passes without seeming to do so. Binny stays beside the woman she doesn't know and polishes her christening cup. There is much to do, much to prepare, much to mend, but it cannot be done in a day and sometimes it is better to do one small thing. She will stay a while longer.

The angel watches with her tinsel wings. Binny wipes and she wipes and she wipes.

The Marriage Manual

Alan and Alice. A textbook marriage. Other couples had come and gone. Divorce, remarriage, several early bereavements, stepchildren, singles' parties, speed-dating ('At our age?' said Alice. 'All I want is a camomile tea.'), but here they were, Alan and Alice, still as one after twenty-three years. The stories they shared had become small legends. 'Do you remember the time . . . ?' Alan would say, and Alice would listen, wide-eyed, smiling, chipping in with a detail or two when he forgot. Their stories were like other people's photograph albums or the family silver, kept in a glass cupboard and taken out for polishing every now and then. They reminded Alan and Alice who they were. And sometimes, yes, as she listened to a neighbour complain about a difficult teenager, or another confessing that she'd had it with her marriage, Alice thought of her home, her husband, her son, and she felt (though she would never admit it) a little smug, a little blessed.

Alan hung his coat in the coat cupboard and placed his

shoes on the rack. Beyond the hall, soft green light pooled from the garden into the conservatory. The Christmas tree twinkled blue, then red, then a joyful combination of both. He reached for the day's post.

No bills, not on Christmas Eve, just a neat pile of opened cards on the hall table. He picked one up, a photographic image of a romantic snow scene. It was the young woman in the red coat again; she seemed to be everywhere. Alan didn't know what it was for, the advert – he couldn't see the connection between the girl with her red coat and the woodland animals that seemed to be following her, and surely she'd be cold in all that snow, but it made him feel festive, especially with the weather so grey and ordinary. He liked the song too that went with the advert on the television. It was catchy.

Alan took a glance at the enormous writing inside the card.

Dear Alice & Alan, Happy Winter Celebration, It's been years!!! Hope you're still alive! Love, as always, Binny, Coco & Luke

'If we don't do it tonight, mister, we never will.'

'Alice?' Alan swung round to find his wife watching him from the conservatory door. She was wearing her mule house-slippers and her slimming slacks, with her cardigan hooked over her shoulders like a pink cape. Her cheeks were flushed and she had straightened her hair so that it hung on either side of her ears like a pressed brown napkin.

'So are you up for it?' she said.

'Are we doing something?'

Alice laughed. 'Don't tell me you've forgotten.'

Alan hoped that if he remained very still and didn't incriminate himself in any way, she would say something that would give him a clue as to what she was talking about.

'Every morning you promise we'll do it and every night you fall asleep. I don't think you've even looked down there.' Alice whipped from her pocket a pair of latex gloves and a ball of polypropylene twine. 'Will's in his room. So come on, Alan. This is your big moment.'

It turned out Alice was referring to Will's Christmas present, ordered in kit form on the internet and stored in a box in the cupboard beneath the stairs. Alan hadn't looked; she was right. He had been putting the job off because it was so easy there would be no fun in it. Assembling a racing bike struck Alan as beneath him, even though it was for their son. Alan would have preferred to make something more challenging on Christmas Eve. An ornamental pond, for instance. He very much wanted to make one of those. But you could not give your twelve-year-old son an ornamental pond for Christmas.

Alice began dragging the box across the hall towards the conservatory. It was far bigger than Alan had expected and clearly also heavier. Her face was on fire with the effort. 'Is it me or is it boiling in here?' she asked, ramming the box into the doorway. 'Allow me,' said Alan. As he slid and shuffled the box into the centre of the conservatory, it gave a tinkly sound like a wind-chime, as if there were tiny pieces inside.

'Maybe something's broken,' Alice said.

'Oh I don't think so.' But even as Alan replied, his heart gave a leap. If something was broken it would need fixing. He parked the box firmly in the centre of the conservatory.

'This is exciting,' said Alice. 'We've never done anything like this together, have we, Alan?' And maybe she was imagining the story that would follow – *the night we built a bike* – because she was beginning to smile.

They studied the box that stood between them. Strange. Alan would have expected a picture, or at the very least a label, and this had neither. It was just a very big and plain brown box, exactly the same as any other, swaddled in strips of brown tape. He used his retractable penknife to carve a small slit in one of the flaps. He lifted it carefully and peered inside.

Every year it seemed harder to find the right Christmas present for Will. When he was small there had been toy animals – a farm set one year, a zoo set another. There had been little plastic knights on horses, followed by soldiers. There had been tractors and aeroplanes, followed by kits to make aeroplanes. But on Christmas morning, Alan would gaze at the pile of presents beneath the tree, decorated by Alice with ribbon in loops and silver bows – she had done a course in gift-wrapping – and instead of feeling excited, he would feel squashed, almost suffocated. Deep down, he knew that no matter what they gave Will, it would be the same, because it was the same every year. Will would open all those professionally gift-wrapped toys one by one, patiently, solemnly peeling off each strip of Sellotape, and he would turn the new toy over and over in his hands, murmur a polite thank-you, and then what would they find him playing with? The ribbon.

'Well?' said Alice, leaning over Alan's shoulder. 'What can you see in the box?'

A soup of small metallic pieces, that was what. Alan had assumed it would just be a case of assembling two alloy wheels. Clearly this was a job for the hand tools. And even though the hall clock was already chiming eight, he felt a tingle of excitement.

'Stand back, Alice,' he said.

Alan shunted the box to its side and tipped its contents over the floor. 'Mind!' she warned, but it was already too late. Hundreds of pieces came crashing and spilling and tumbling forth like water from a spring. Nuts and bolts and washers and screws, caps and catches and metal plates, as well as piping, tubing, brackets and clamps, all gushing and skittering across the conservatory floor towards the three-piece suite and the Christmas tree.

'Blimey,' said Alan.

'Goodness,' said Alice. She dropped to her knees. The open box was almost twice her size. 'Is it normally like this? Where are the wheels?'

'I don't know, Alice. I can't even see a chain.'

'Are we expected to make all those things ourselves?'

Alan scratched his head. 'I guess,' he said. 'I guess.'

'The instructions must be in the box.' Alice crawled towards it. Alan went to fetch his toolset from the kitchen.

Alan was what Alice affectionately called a DIY *nut*. He had begun with the basics when they first moved in – putting up a picture hook, a set of shelves, followed by small repair jobs, and over the years he had taught himself bigger things. How to replace internal doors, insulate the roof, build radiator covers and plumb in a simple basin. Theirs was the first house along the avenue to have security lamps (installed by Alan), as well as green-backlit shrubbery with ten different mood settings (also Alan's work). He had fitted the downstairs bathroom with one of those show-time mirrors – though there had been a minor incident with the wiring and Alice still preferred the one upstairs – and once he had surprised her with a brand-new kitchen. Last summer, instead of going on holiday, Alan had built the Edwardian-style conservatory. It had been the best summer Alan could remember. Every day, instead of dressing in shorts and a Hawaiian shirt, he had put on his hi-vis jacket and a hard hat. The conservatory was his number-one achievement. There were moments during its construction when he had wanted to give up, when the job had seemed too big and he knew he was out of his depth, but Alan had worked it out, every detail. (True, he had had to make some adjustments of his own, because these kits were never perfect.) Sometimes he liked to inspect the white plastic-coated frame, the polycarbonate roof panels, the smooth silicone joins, not because there was anything wrong, but just because he loved to be reminded that he had fitted them all by himself.

When he returned to the conservatory, it was silent.

'Alice?' he called, but there was no sign of her, only the box and all those tiny pieces; perhaps she'd decided to leave the kit to him. Alan rolled up his sleeves and picked up a screwdriver and found himself humming the catchy Christmas song that went with that advert . . .

'Nice singing, Alan.'

He froze. 'Alice?' She was not in the room. No one was.

'I can't seem to find the instructions,' said the box, quite high-pitched.

Alice reversed, mule-heels first, from its opening. She crunched with her hands and knees over several nuts and bolts and fished out a small item that looked like a stub axle. Alan rushed towards her.

'Let me do this,' he said, more enthusiastically than he intended, taking up a central sitting position on the floor. 'Why don't you find me things?'

'I thought I was going to *help* this time? I thought we were building this together?'

'But you're so good at finding things. You can start with the spanner.'

Alice opened the toolbox. She passed him his spanner.

'Just as well I know what I'm doing. By the time I was Will's age, I could dismantle and rebuild my bicycle at the drop of a hat. I'll have the wrench now.'

'Wrench. Voilà.'

'That's another ring spanner.'

'Is it?'

'It is.'

'They all look the same, Alan.'

He laughed indulgently. He knew his tools like old friends. Alan outlined the differences between an open-ended spanner, a ring spanner and an adjustable one, including their different functions and sizes, and Alice nipped her hand to her mouth to dispose of a small yawn. Whilst he matched three bolts with three nuts, Alice crawled back inside the box to have another look for the instructions.

It was a disappointment that Alan couldn't get Will interested in DIY. It was what fathers and sons did. They built things, and once they'd finished, they drove to specialist shops and looked at new tools with which to build the same things all over again, only slightly better. Alan had tried with Will. 'Shall we make a set of shelves, son? How about I show you how to use the electric drill?' But Will stared back at him with his unsettling deep-brown eyes and his long hair tucked behind his ears and those tiny shoulders like a bunch of twigs. There was something so impenetrable about him. 'For God's sake,' Alan would snap. 'Why can't you get a haircut?'

'Aha!' cried Alice from inside the box. 'I've found the instructions. They were tucked inside the flap.'

Alan had expected a leaflet, but what she had found was a black manual. It looked more like a hymn book than a set of instructions for a kit.

'I'd better take a look,' he said. Alice was already flicking through the pages, her face bunched into a frown.

'It doesn't seem to be in English, Alan. It doesn't even have pictures.' She pushed the book towards him.

She was right. What language was this? It was page upon page of curlicues and swirls. It looked more like musical notes than letters, wearing pointed hats and shoes.

'So how are we supposed to make a bicycle if we have no idea what to do?' she asked. She was almost on the verge of tears. 'Why did you leave this so late, Alan?'

There was nothing for it but to be practical. Use his common sense. He rooted through the nuts and bolts, efficiently pairing them together.

Alice knelt at his side, her hands twitching in her lap. 'Are you sure I can't do anything?'

'I think I should just get us started. Ratchet, please.'

'You said we would do this together. What is a ratchet?'

'*This* is a ratchet, Alice. Do I have to do everything?'

'No, Alan. You could let me help. Like we agreed . . .'

'Once I've got the skeleton of the thing, that's when you can do all the detailed work. I mean, you're marvellous at the detail, Alice. Look at the soft furnishings. Detail is where you come into your own.'

Alice inspected her fingernails. She blew out an impatient sigh. She flattened the tips of her hair and sighed again. She cast her eyes over the room. 'Alan?' she asked. 'Is that a new crack?'

'What?' He was too busy to look.

'Behind you. Where you knocked through to build the conservatory.'

'Of course not. If you could just hold this piece – whoa now, gently – Alice? Alice? What are you doing? Why aren't you helping me? Where are you going?'

The clock chimed nine.

Alice stood with her face to the wall. She was right about the new crack. It reached – now she examined it – from the picture rail at the top, down to the floor tiles. It hadn't been there before. She'd have noticed when she was vacuuming. There was definitely a hairline split in the plaster just at the point where the outer panel of the conservatory met the external brickwork of the house. She pressed her cheeks against it. It felt strangely soothing, like a cold hand. She could even hear something – what was it?

57

– a small sad sigh, as if something was travelling towards her from very far away.

'Alice!' called Alan. 'Alice! Spanner!'

'Get it yourself!'

Alice gave a start. She never snapped. And she'd worked so hard over the years to lose her estuary vowels, but here they were all over again. She had barely voiced those consonants.

'I beg your pardon?' said Alan.

'I'm TireD,' she said carefully (sounding more like Alice). 'I'm TireD of passing things. I wanT to helP.'

'There was no need to be rude,' said Alan (sounding exactly like himself). 'You wouldn't have spoken to me like that at the student union. The night we first met.' He laughed. 'Don't you remember?'

Alice squinted at the crack in the wall. She could have sworn it gave a shiver. 'I was drunk.'

'Drunk? You? I don't think so . . .'

'Yup. Completely trolleyed.'

'*Alice?*'

'Pissed as a fart. Smashed.'

'I beg your pardon?'

Alan laughed again, but it no longer sounded like happy laughter. 'You weren't drunk. It was love at first sight. You saw me and you ran into my arms. "My, you're great,"

58

you said. Come on, Alice – you know this story. You had that funny accent I could never understand. Remember?'

A dart of cold air shot from the crack in the wall straight to Alice's mouth. 'Mind your *feet*, I said! I was trying to get to the loo! Mind your honking great, winkle-pickered, who-do-you-think-you're-kidding feet! You were standing in my way! Even in our wedding photographs you were standing in my way! Not to mention when you finally got me to the hospital and the midwife yelled at me to push!' Alice slammed her hands to her mouth.

Alan was staring up at her from the floor and he wasn't laughing, happily or otherwise. 'What did you just say?' He sounded winded.

Alice fumbled behind her for the settee and lowered herself on to it. Her knee joints felt weak and her cheeks were aflame. What had happened to her mouth? She reached for a tiny thing that looked as if it might fit on to another tiny thing, if she just pressed them together, very slowly and deliberately. 'I'll work on this bit, shall I?'

'But that's our *story*,' said Alan. 'We've always talked about how we met at the student union. How you ran into my arms and it was love at first sight.' He picked up a screwdriver. 'Though now you mention it, it's only fair to add I had my eye on someone else.'

'*You?*' she said, in a disbelieving way that he didn't quite like. 'Who?'

'A young lady called Linda Spiers.'

'Linda Spiers? Not *the* Linda Spiers? She had breasts the size of my head.'

'She found me very entertaining.'

'Well, well,' Alice said tightly. 'I had no idea.' She placed the tiny thing inside a pair of pliers and tried to wedge the pliers between her knees. They jumped out and bit her fingers. 'Oh,' she cried, dropping everything, 'this stupid *thing* won't go on to *this* stupid thing.'

'That is because they don't, Alice. They are both washers. So hang on, what are we saying here?'

'I don't know.'

If only the kit was not so complicated. If only the instructions made some sense. If only they'd bought a bike from a shop, all grown-up and ready-made. She wasn't even sure Will wanted a bike, not really. Who knew what he wanted? As a little boy he had been so happy, so inquisitive. He had followed her everywhere, constantly chattering. These days she was lucky if she got so much as a hello. It was like talking to a person who was not there.

She suspected he was being bullied at school. She watched him walk up the garden path every afternoon, his head so low it looked too heavy for his shoulders, and she felt pulled apart. Only a few weeks ago she'd had a meeting with his head of year, Miss King, a cherry-faced woman, possibly because she was zipped to the chin in a brand-new puffy skiing jacket. Alice had explained all about Will's silence, his frequent headaches, how he wasn't himself any more. Miss King had listened carefully and then she had asked such terrible questions Alice had felt ill; she had actually felt assaulted. 'I think Will is going through a period of adjustment,' Miss King had finally said. And she had given Alice a steady, meaningful look that implied . . . *what*?

Alice had no idea. She'd fled before she could work it out.

But that was not the point. Alan was still talking. He was still going over the night when they first met. 'It seems to me that what we're saying is that contrary to the story we have always told, it was not love at first sight. Our meeting was, in fact, a very ordinary accident. Alice?'

She abandoned the washers. Instead she arranged nuts and bolts across the carpet in order of size. Small ones; very small ones; tiny ones; teeny-weeny ones.

'I'd like to know the truth,' said Alan.

'Can we just finish this thing?' said Alice.

Something in the conservatory gave a snap.

*

61

Alan prowled with his torch through the green-lit shrubbery. He had an uneasy feeling, as if the ground had suddenly been swished away beneath his feet. He inspected the patio, and then slowly swung the beam of his torch across the conservatory. The room was empty, save for the flashing Christmas tree and the hundreds of pieces and the very large box. There was no sign of structural disturbance. Everything was intact. And reaching forward to touch the cool white plastic-covered frame, Alan too felt solid again.

If only the weather would do something. You couldn't say it was warm, but it wasn't cold either. It was nothing. Colourless skies all day that threatened rain but never brought it, that just hung around loutishly, and low dark cloud at night that sat between the land and the sky like a piece of wadding. All along the avenue the houses pulsed with Christmas lights. No wonder people decorated everything they could lay their hands on with sparkles and baubles like shiny fruit; how else to get through the endless days of dark and cloud? But the truth was that sometimes, very occasionally, Alan had a queasy feeling about Christmas, as if it was just about adding way too many things so that one could enjoy the relief of removing them all again, come January.

He touched the conservatory walls one more time. No, Alice was wrong. There was no crack.

Glancing up, Alan was startled to catch a small face peering out from Will's bedroom window. It looked the loneliest thing. Despite the mild night, Alan shivered and pulled his jacket close. And then the face was gone.

'The noise stopped,' called Alice. 'The windows gave a brief rattle and that was the end of it. I suppose it was a bird.'

'Probably,' said Alan. He placed his shoes back on the rack and padded through to the conservatory.

Alice was kneeling on the floor amidst the mess of nuts and bolts, engrossed in trying to screw one piece on to another. Her make-up bag was open beside her; she'd applied a new layer of face powder to her red-hot cheeks but they still glowed. One of her straightened sections of hair had also sprung into a zig-zag of curls, right at the back where she couldn't see. He felt a tug of tenderness.

She said, 'I went upstairs to check on Will.'

'Was he all right?'

'Fast asleep.'

The clock chimed ten.

Alan crouched on the floor beside Alice. He had a child-like longing to take hold of her hand – he knew it so well, after all, he had seen the skin grow older, he had seen it begin to slacken and crease, but at that moment he felt he knew and loved her hand more than he had ever loved it.

Instead he reached for a titanium bolt and screwed it diligently to a plate.

She said into the stillness, 'I don't know what came over me, Alan. All that nonsense about the night we met. I think it's this kit. All these pieces and no instructions. Of course I was attracted to you.'

'It was the same for me. Linda Spiers had nothing on you.'

Now they laughed, familiar easy laughter that felt like sitting in comfy chairs.

'Shall I pass you something, Alan?'

'You don't need to pass me anything, Alice.'

'Oh, I like passing you things.'

'You could pass me the flat-head screwdriver. If you wanted to.'

'I would love that.' She fetched him another wrench, but he didn't say anything, he just smiled.

'We have so many stories, Alice. What about the time I surprised you with the fitted kitchen?'

'Oh,' she said, remembering and laughing. 'Now that *was* a story.'

For several minutes they worked in silence. He knew she must be thinking about the fitted kitchen because every now and then she gave a small, breathy laugh and shook her head. Then she said, 'Would you mind passing me the slanted tweezers?'

'I beg your pardon?'

'From my make-up bag. I can't get a grip with these pointed ones.'

Alan turned. 'Exactly what tools are you using?'

'While you were outside, I realized your tools are too big for my hands. That was the problem. So I fetched my make-up bag and – ta da – I have made a pedal.' She held up something that looked like a mangled plate.

'And where exactly on the instructions does it show you how to make a pedal?'

'It doesn't. It doesn't say anything, if you remember. We are building a bicycle with no idea how it is supposed to fit together. The only instructions we have seem to be written in scribble. So I have put this bit on this bit, and voilà.'

'But they don't fit together. They have only fitted together because you have rammed one into the other with a make-up brush.'

'Heated tongs.'

'For crying out loud!'

Alice threw down her pedal and returned to the wall. She could have sworn the crack gave a hiss. 'For your information, this has got worse,' she said.

Alan shook his head. 'It's just the plaster,' he said. 'All buildings move. It's because we've had no rain.'

If Alice put her eye to it, she could actually see inside the crack. It was dark and deep. She worked her fingernail into the widest point. Dust as soft as cornflour and tiny grit stones crumbled free. Alice felt that bitter shot of sleety air again. 'And anyway, I may not be any good at DIY, but at least I've never forgotten to buy you a Christmas present.'

The sentence hit Alan like a slap. 'Alice, that was fourteen years ago. It's water under the bridge. I gave you the fitted kitchen as a surprise. We were only just talking about that. You said it was the best Christmas present ever.'

'I was being kind. I wanted perfume. Nice underwear. Normal things. Not granite worktops. Not saloon doors. I don't even like cooking.'

'You cook all the time.'

'That doesn't mean I like it. I'm a slave to the kitchen—'

'What you are forgetting is that you were extremely depressed fourteen years ago. It wasn't easy.'

'Are you saying it was *my* fault you forgot to buy me a Christmas present?' Oh no, she was shouting again.

Alan snatched up a cable luber and tried to find something with which to match it. No sign, of course, of any cable. He glanced at Alice slumped against the wall, all pink, another section of her hair spriggy with curls. There *was* a crack, he could see that now, but she was only making matters worse by sticking her fingers inside it. He felt a twist of anger as if someone had pinched his bowels. He reached for the hammer and several nails.

'What I should have said – *bang* – what I wanted to say – was, One: Buck up your ideas! Two: Get a job if you're so lonely! *Bang*. You haven't worked since you got a degree! Three: Have you any idea what it's like to come home every night to a self-appointed martyr to domestic appliances? *Bang*. Four: For your information, you cannot cook! I have spent years – *bang* – years! with fish bones stuck between my teeth and chewing on gristle and burning with indigestion! You undercook meat! You over-cook vegetables! Your puddings are enough to give a man a heart attack! I didn't forget your present that year. I just couldn't be bothered to think of one!'

Alice felt made of air. Even as she heard the words, she thought she was mishearing. He couldn't really be saying those things, could he? She reached for the wall and instead found the crack again. She dug her fingers right inside the crevice and felt the cold. It shifted and stretched, as if something were trying to get out. If she didn't hold on tight, she was certain she would slither to the floor.

'Is that really true?' she asked.

Alan huffed and huffed again.

'Could you really not be bothered to buy me a present?' Her chin trembled and she took deep breaths so she wouldn't cry, but in the patchy silence that followed, something else happened instead. Anger. Where was it coming from? It filled her like shards of ice, as if her arms and head and feet were all freezing up and turning to glass. '*I wanted a baby!*'

'Alice, calm down,' said Alan.

'Don't tell me to calm down!' said Alice.

'It wasn't my fault you couldn't conceive.'

'Oh, ha ha ha!'

'What is *that* supposed to mean?'

Alice had no idea. But at that moment she was so angry she couldn't think. 'I should have gone,' she spat. 'I should have gone the day I packed my suitcase.'

'You packed a suitcase? When?' Alan wasn't so much screwing things together any more as wedging them into blocks and chucking them aside.

'On our tenth wedding anniversary.'

'You packed a suitcase on our tenth wedding anniversary? But that was the year before you had Will –'

'I know!' Her pulse was thudding so hard she felt light-headed, she almost couldn't keep up with it, but there was an awful pleasure too, a kind of relief – almost hot it was so cold – in speaking the words. 'I wanted to leave you.'

The silence was broken only by the clanking of a hammer.

'So why didn't you?'

'I got a cold.'

Alan's throat tightened. He could barely swallow. He was about to shout, he would have shouted, but instead the polycarbonate roof panels above their heads gave a long creaking moan like a wooden ship at sea. Their eyes shot upwards. And then their heads swivelled left and right as all around them the silicone joins hissed and the glass walls rattled. The crack in the wall stretched as if yawning.

'Keep calm,' shouted Alan, leaping to his feet. He held out his arms, warning everything to stay in place.

'Calm?' shrieked Alice. '*Calm?* The conservatory's *falling down*! I'm going to check on Will.'

'I'll come with you.'

She turned. Her face was red as a panic button. 'You're the one who built it! You stay here and sort out this mess!' Alice kicked off her mule slippers and fled towards the stairs.

Everything was exactly as usual on the first-floor landing. Not one sign of disturbance. You could be up here and have no clue about the mayhem below. Lamps shone a buttery yellow over the flowered wallpaper. Will's Christmas stocking hung from the handle of his closed door. Alice knocked quietly. More a *tap, tap* than a knock. She eased the door open, just a few inches.

Will lay fast asleep, tucked on one side, his head clasped between his hands.

Everything was so much easier when he was asleep. It was the only time these days when she truly stopped worrying.

Alice crept past his bed to the window and parted the curtain. She could see right down into the conservatory. Alan was back on the floor, screwing pieces together like a madman, his hair sticking out in tufty patches. All around him the garden glowed lime-cordial green.

Perhaps it was because she was looking down on Alan or perhaps it was to do with the strange night, but set there against the darkness, a middle-aged man in a glass conservatory – even if he was backlit by his own green shrubbery – seemed such a small thing. Everything did. Everything seemed so small and fragile, as if it were made of wet tissue paper and might disintegrate at any moment. Fleetingly Alice pictured the young woman she had once been, who reeked of rose oil and was going to travel the world with a rucksack. She remembered Binny, the girl she had followed everywhere, the way they would lie on the grass and laugh for hours, smoking Binny's mother's Sobranie cocktail cigarettes. And now look at me, she thought. I'm half of something, but I am not a whole. If we met, Binny and I, she wouldn't even know me.

Alice had other friends, of course. But how did you say to them, those friends, those women she'd passed on the avenue with pushchairs and bags of shopping, those women she'd helped when washing machines packed up or sugar ran out, how did you say, I think my marriage might be – *what*? What was the word for what her marriage had become? Not *over*. Not that. But what?

Different.

Not the thing she had expected when she started.

And then how did you say to your friends, I think my son might be – *what*? What might he be? She remembered the way Miss King had spoken to her at the school. The questions she'd asked. Was Will happy at home? Were there difficulties? Was everything in his parents' relationship as it should be? Of course he was happy at home! It was school that was the problem! Will was very happy at school, the infuriating Miss King had replied. He was always laughing. Always the centre of things. Everyone adored him. 'But sometimes we don't see what is under our noses,' Miss King had observed, not looking at Alice, but straightening the zipper on her jacket. 'I think Will is going through a period of adjustment.'

Alice thought again of the way Miss King had lifted her gaze suddenly, her eyes unblinking, as if she had given the important cue and was now waiting for Alice to speak her line.

The clock chimed eleven. She should go back downstairs. At the door, she turned. Suddenly she had an odd feeling, no more than a hunch, that Will was watching. That he'd been watching all evening. She closed the door quickly, brushing her hand against the felt stocking on the handle, and heard something rustle.

Dear Santa. For Christmas I would like . . .

Alice read with her mouth open.

'Alan?' She stood at the doorway of the conservatory, Will's letter in her hand. 'I've got something to tell you.'

Alan had fitted most of the pieces together now. The kit was taking shape – sections were almost a foot in length. Carefully he lifted the largest piece and balanced it upright. As he removed his hands, she held her breath, transfixed, but it only gave a small unsteady wobble like a child taking to its feet for the first time, and remained standing.

'Will doesn't want a racing bike for Christmas,' she said.

'That's maybe just as well,' said Alan.

Meanwhile the crack in the wall had become almost an opening; you could have stuffed a tight roll of newspaper inside it. A pool of powdered grey cement lay on the floor. And Alice was certain, now she looked, that the pitched roof was not so much pitched any more as buckling. 'Are you absolutely sure this conservatory is safe?' she asked.

'Would I be sitting here if I didn't think it was safe?'

Nevertheless there was something disjointed about Alan too, surrounded by all those tiny pieces. There was something disjointed about everything.

Alice held out Will's Christmas letter. 'He says he wants a dress. A green one. With a sweetheart neckline and a ribbon belt. Also a pack of Top Trump cards and a memory stick. I've got both of those. Just not the dress. I didn't . . . you know. I didn't think of that.' Alice stooped for a screw, only instead of pairing it with a nut, she cradled it in her palm.

Alan slammed one stretch of tubing into another, but somehow he missed and they both leapt out of his hands and shot towards the Christmas tree. The crack in the wall gave a low murmur and spat out a shower of freezing dust.

Alice dropped the screw and clung to the doorframe. Oh, here came that cold, screaming feeling again.

'Do you *think*,' she said fiercely, 'do you *really think* you're any *good* at DIY? The number of times, the number of *times*, I've had to call out a *proper builder* once you were at a safe distance from the house! And what about the time you fitted showtime mirror lights in the bathroom and practically *fried* me? You should be *locked up* for the damage you've done!'

Alan leapt to his feet, brandishing a wrench and one of Alice's make-up brushes. 'You think you're a *slave* to the home? The house is filthy. It's a *tip*! I have to take my clothes to the cleaners after you've washed them! You — *Essex girl*!'

'You — *financial adviser*!'

A green lightning ball seemed to shoot through the crack in the wall and skipped across the floor, striking the Christmas tree and felling it with a bang as if it had been shot execution-style through the heart. The metal supports of the conservatory twisted and buckled. Alan charged towards Alice and lifted her into the safety of the hallway just as the polycarbonate roof panels gave a ripping noise and split. There was a sound of cracking and snapping as the outer supports lifted and then, one by one, the sides of the conservatory popped open and peeled outwards like a pack of cards. *Plink, plank, plonk.* It took barely seconds to fall, but in doing so, it must have cut short the power supply because the green-lit shrubbery was suddenly not green any more but night-coloured. There was nothing but the bitter smell of burnt electrical wires.

'Alan?' said Alice.

'Alice?' said Alan.

Alan and Alice stepped through the gap in the wall. The side of the house was a wound letting in the night and where there had been a conservatory there were only empty frames and layer upon layer of rubble and plastic roofing. Strands of silicone hung in streamers.

'What have we said?' Alice wrapped her arms around her body like a belt. 'What have we done?' She stared into the dark.

The truth was, there were no instructions when you got married. There was no manual in the birthing suite that explained how to bring up a happy child. No one said, you do this, and then you do this, and after that this will happen. You made it up as you went along. And the people who had brought you up were no use either. They seemed to have completely forgotten what they'd done to make things work. How a couple stayed together or brought up a child was anyone's guess. But just because it was not the thing you'd expected did not necessarily mean it had not worked.

Alan and Alice stood silent and side by side.

*

The hall clock chimed midnight. Once more, Will took up his watching post at the bedroom window. He had seen everything. He always did; he was always watching. But now something was different. What was it?

There was no conservatory.

Two stooped figures stepped into the black nothingness below. One was his mother, her hair all curly, and the other his father, covered in dust. Will saw his father's hand grope its passage around his mother's waist. He saw her head lower like a drawbridge to rest on his father's shoulder.

Will took a good look at the present his parents had made. It had a leaning spire and two small wheels like hands and a set of flappers that kept it upright. Its body was a tower of ill-matched nuts and screws. Caught over one shoulder was his father's jacket and at its feet were thrown his mother's mules. It seemed to grow out of the wreckage like a wild flower on a bombsite. He was glad it wasn't a bicycle. Will liked it. He liked it very much.

And in that moment Will knew something. It was so big and strange, this thing, he barely had the words for it. It was only a thought really, a shape. Long after his father had gone, and his mother too, there would be this. This whatever it was. This fact. His parents had put him together with the chaos of their loving. They had done their best and they had made mistakes, yes, and most of the time it was no more than a botch-job, and now those mistakes were a part of who he was. But he had been loved, he *was* loved, and he too could love. Take courage, Will.

Overhead an aeroplane passed, its lights blinking in the dark. Will watched for a while, and as he looked he noticed another and another and another, like stars. He imagined all those people inside the planes, some sleeping, some awake, some staring down at the ground below, seeing house lights and street lamps and maybe even the houses on the avenue. All those people flying to wherever they were going for Christmas. Each of them so different, but travelling above him, all the same.

Will looked up, and at the same moment he saw himself looking down, as if he had just passed himself and said hello.

Then a soft wind picked up and wiped the sky clean.

Christmas Day at the Airport

It is early Christmas morning at the airport. All flights have been suspended until further notice. Nothing is landing and nothing is taking off.

Travellers gather beneath the departures board and gaze upwards. It's like waiting for a sign, only in this case nothing happens. All these people, some dressed for skiing holidays, some for a break in the sun, others in casual clothing for a long-haul flight. There is no seating left. People sleep at tables with heads in their hands and sprawl on the floor, using coats and rucksacks as makeshift blankets and pillows. Suitcases stand like garden walls between one group and another. It is not yet fully light outside. The airport eateries are already running low on food.

Magda stands in stillness. She wears jogging pants and a loose hoodie that sits over her belly. Her hair is pinched into a ponytail and it hangs like the scrappiest bit of rag. Magda, too, is waiting for a sign, only hers is a different kind, and she has no idea how it will come, whether it will be a feeling or a smell or maybe something she hasn't even known before. Something she doesn't yet have a word for. Once when she was a child she saw a deer in the middle of the road and she thinks of it now, with its nose to the air, its haunches frozen, in the grip of fear. She has never seen a deer since.

The thickset woman at her side wears a denim boiler suit and nickel bracelets that hang with the weight of chains. Her arms and neck are blue with tattoos: painted birds and mermaids and dragons. You wouldn't know but on her back she has a painted warrior with hair to her waist; Magda loves that. It's like looking at a painting in a museum. The woman is almost twice her age, old enough to be her mother, and her hair is dyed punk-pink and shaved to fuzz. Passers-by give the two women a wide berth. Trailer trash, someone mutters. Well, so what? They've heard worse.

The departure lounge is so polished and shiny it could be made of glass. It is reflected in the windows, even more brilliant and doubled in size, spread across the early-morning light as if it were made of water. Everywhere there are flashing signs and reduced-price duty-free gift ideas. The air smells of coffee and a thousand perfumes. From a giant screen, the same short film keeps playing on a loop, something to do with a young woman walking through snow and some little animals, only they are not real, not like the young woman in her red coat, they are cartoon animals, with exaggerated ears and fluffy tails like pom-poms and buck teeth that give them a cute look. It must an advert for something, because everything here is an advert for something, but the girl can't imagine what. It's like a no man's land, this place. You could lose yourself.

The girl scans the lists of destinations – places she has never visited: Palma, Reus, Enfidha – and they are each coupled with the words 'DELAYED. Awaiting Information'.

'There's freak weather coming,' a middle-aged man says to his wife. They both wear linen suits, white with a crease in them, and straw hats, and they speak very loudly, the way Magda has noticed that some English people do, as if no one else is present. 'Nothing taking off. Nothing landing. We could be here for hours. Merry bloody Christmas.'

Someone says there's been a terrorist attack and someone else says there hasn't, it's just a problem with the computers at air-traffic control.

'Whatever it is, we're not going anywhere,' repeats the man in his linen suit. He tears his straw hat off his head as if to show that is the end of his holiday.

'You sure you're OK, Mags?' asks the older woman.

'I think so,' says Magda.

'You don't look it.'

'I am OK.'

Later, Magda overhears some people talking about snow and others about flash floods, but they are still there, all of them waiting in the departure lounge. If anything, there are more people now; this is not a huge airport.

'You want anything?' asks the older woman. They use simple English words because the older woman knows no Latvian and Magda knows no Romanian.

Magda shakes her head. 'Something's happening.'

'What?'

'I don't know.'

She thinks again of that deer and the way every muscle of it was waiting.

Not all the passengers at the airport are people. The animal reception centre is a white building situated a stone's throw from the departure lounge where pets are held until they can be collected by their owners. The staff take care of animal welfare during shipment, help to stop smuggling, and X-ray animals to check for drugs and bombs.

This morning there is a lively smell of farmyard mixed with the more familiar one of detergent. You get it as soon as you pass Security. Manure and bleach, thinks Mrs Pike, deputy manager, arriving for the first shift of Christmas Day. She says to one of the girls (she can never tell them apart, and when she does, the girls only go and dye their hair blue or purple or pink, and Mrs Pike is confused all over again), she says, 'I am certain I can smell manure.' Hester. That is her name. Or at least that is what it says on the plastic identity badge hanging from a ribbon around her neck.

'Oh, that will be the donkey,' says Hester. She seems to have green hair.

'What donkey?' says Mrs Pike.

'The donkey that came in the night,' says Hester. 'It has no paperwork.'

'A donkey?'

Hester makes an infuriating 'Uh-huh' noise at her mobile phone. She doesn't even glance up.

'Why did no one mention a donkey before?'

'I guess they thought you'd notice. There's a goat and four cheetahs as well.'

Mrs Pike gropes for the edge of the desk. 'A goat? *Cheetahs?* We're only supposed to have cats and dogs.'

'And fish,' points out Hester. Her hair hangs like grass.

'And fish,' concedes Mrs Pike, reaching for her handbag and tugging out her Nicorettes.

'The cheetahs don't have their microchips. We are holding them until a convenient alternative can be found. Nobody has a clue about the goat. It's a total nightmare.'

Christmas Morning. A strange weather front is

apparently heading in the direction of the airport. The computers have gone down in air-traffic control. Cars are at a standstill on the two-mile stretch from the motorway. Nobody can move; Mrs Pike had to abandon her Polo and walk. At home she still has the turkey to stuff, along with a vegan alternative, because at six p.m. her three daughters will arrive, along with her two sons-in-law and her six Pikelet grandchildren. The last thing Mrs Pike needs or wants is a grassy-haired girl telling her about four cheetahs without microchips, an unexplained goat and a donkey.

'Also a terrapin,' says Hester. 'A guy was trying to smuggle it through in his underpants.'

'All I need really is to lie down,' says Magda. Her friend watches her with as much fear in her eyes as Magda has ever seen.

'It's not coming, is it?'

'I don't think so, Jo.'

Magda isn't in pain, not as such, but she can feel the baby inside her, and for the first time she doesn't seem big enough to hold it. There is a small person bundled like a stowaway in her belly, poking and fidgeting, growing. 'I'm OK,' she says, because the older woman is standing with her body stooped and her big, thick arms outstretched, as if bracing herself to catch a rugby ball.

'I'll ask someone to move, Mags,' she says. 'So you can lie down.'

'Don't worry, Jo.' The girl doesn't want to go drawing attention to herself. Besides, everyone looks so cross and miserable, there is no point asking. She just wants to be alone, just her and the baby. She doesn't even need Johanna. Not right now.

'I will ask, though,' Johanna says, and then Magda doesn't hear any more because here is that wrenching feeling and she has to breathe into it, right into the eye of it, so that it doesn't split her open. She notices Johanna has gone and then she feels another wave of wrenching and she forgets Johanna. She forgets everything. She is just a tiny body with a huge hollowing punch inside. By the time it's over, Jo is back.

'You were right,' Johanna says. 'No one wants to give up their seat. We need to find you somewhere else.' Fear makes her voice sound younger and smaller than the rest of her. Magda wants to hold her, like she does at home, Johanna's head in her lap while she strokes her pink cropped hair and feels how soft it is beneath her fingertips, but people will look and so she can't.

The baby is still, but soon it will be pushing her again. The moment of calm is even more precious because already it has an end. 'I only need to be somewhere quiet,' she says. She thinks she can hear choral music, but how can that be? It must be in her head.

There is nothing for it but to sing. 'O Come All Ye Faithful.' What else can you do if you are the Stroud Girls' Choir and you are wearing embroidered blue sweatshirts that tell everybody you are the Stroud Girls' Choir and you are stuck at the airport, with no room to swing a cat?

'Come along, girls,' interrupts Shelley. 'Chins up.'

'What about Winston, Miss?'

'What about him?' says Shelley. Winston, her sixteen-year-old son, is sitting on his travelling bag with his face in his hands and his blue sweatshirt wrapped like a turban around his scalp. He has a headache.

'Does Winston have to put his chin up an' all?'

'Yes,' says Shelley. 'Winston?'

Winston staggers to his feet and puts up his chin. The girls are all a good year younger than him but he barely reaches their shoulders. Shelley lifts her hands for silence.

She hasn't slept for worry. Her head is hammering. Last time she took the choir on tour, it was supposed to be lights-out at nine-thirty. Instead she spent every night trying to barricade all fifteen members of the Stroud Girls' Choir into the fourth floor of their motel. She put Winston in charge so that she could grab a bite to eat and later found him tied to a chair whilst all fifteen choir members knocked back vodka and pineapple juice in the bar. After the tour there was an additional bill for broken toilets, a jammed sink, the dismantling of a Teasmade and the theft of fifteen waitress uniforms. She had sworn never to take the Stroud Girls' Choir anywhere ever again, not even down to the shopping mall for a lunchtime sing-song, and then they went and won both the local and national heats for Girls' Choir of the Year. It was hard to believe they had been invited to battle it out on the banks of Lake Geneva in the European finals just after Christmas. But they had. The competition would open with a gala performance by all finalists on Boxing Day.

Johanna asks everyone. The answer is always the same. No, they will not give up their seat. 'But my wife,' she says in her broken English. 'She is pregnant.' Well, that only makes it worse. People won't even catch her eye when they hear that.

'You should go home,' someone tells her, and she doesn't know whether he means back to the flat or Eastern Europe.

The baby is due in six weeks. Magda is not supposed to fly, not at this stage, but the tickets were cheap last-minute ones so they kept quiet about her pregnancy. There are legal documents that Johanna needs to sign, relating to the sale of her mother's house in Bucharest. She is walking fast, past the rows of shops. It's hard to keep her mind focussed when there are so many people and so many things to buy. She wants to know what is happening to Magda and whether it's normal, but she has no idea who to ask. She isn't even sure she has the right words. 'Watch where you're going!' someone shouts. She looks to her left and realizes it's Father Christmas.

Six of them, actually. They are drinking cans of Coke outside Duty-Free.

'Have you seen any kids?' asks another of the Father Christmases.

'Kids?' repeats Johanna.

'We're looking for kids. We're the entertainment. We've been laid on by the airport authority. Until things get sorted in this place.'

One of the Father Christmases has lost his white beard, or maybe he has chosen not to wear it. His skin is dark and soft and he looks all of eighteen.

Johanna points in the direction of the seats. 'Lots of children there,' she says.

The Father Christmases give her a thumbs-up and swagger away, ringing sleigh bells and shouting, 'HO, HO, HO!' They sound more like a bunch of hungry football fans than bringers of gifts and good tidings. Briefly she wonders about the father of Magda's baby. It's a painful question and it still hurts like a spike every time it sneaks up on her.

Let's face it, he could be anyone. Magda was already pregnant when she and Johanna first met. The father of her baby could be anywhere. He could be right here at the airport, for all Johanna knows. 'What do you mean, you don't remember?' she had asked, over and over. Sometimes the question seemed to ask itself. All Magda remembered was that she'd been at a party. She'd been given a drink. That was all. When she came round she was in a garden, she didn't even know whose, and she was half-dressed with a punched-up eye.

For a while Johanna had felt betrayed. Eaten up with jealousy. She knew she had no reason to feel either of these things – the two women hadn't even known each other when Magda had gone to the party – but it was the thought of someone else, a man, fetching her a drink, leading her to the door, kissing her mouth. ('You *must* remember something, Magda!' 'I don't. I don't.') If only Magda would show some anger, but she never did. 'You don't have to have this baby,' Johanna had told her. It wasn't the sixties. What happened was rape. 'And you know,' she'd shouted, hurting with the memory of other children she had known, half-starved, beaten up regularly, some of them, 'it's *wrong* to have a baby you don't want.'

And Magda had looked back at her with soft grey eyes and said, 'But I do, Jo. I want this baby with you.' Johanna had asked Magda to marry her. She knew, even then, that she would never love anyone else.

Johanna feels a pang of sickness, then realizes it's hunger. She should buy Magda a drink and some food. Maybe that's the problem; they haven't eaten since last night. Johanna had assumed they'd be in the air by now. She heads towards Duty-Free.

'No,' the assistant tells her, 'you can't buy just one bar of chocolate. You can only purchase dis special Christmas bumper pack.' It is about the length and thickness of Johanna's arm. Johanna buys bottled water and the chocolate. It's cripplingly expensive; normally they would spend the same amount on a week's groceries.

'Do you want da fluffy toy?' asks the assistant. She seems to be dressed as an angel with a tinsel halo and she has such a bad cold she has lost the use of her nose.

'What fluffy toy?'

'Da penguins are all sold out,' says the assistant. 'We've only got lambs left. You get da fluffy toy free with da chocolate. It's a bargain.'

'Could I leave the fluffy toy and pay not so much money for the chocolate?'

The assistant scowls as if Johanna has just done something offensive, like breaking into her native tongue. A woman behind her, who is dressed from head to toe in brand-new snow gear, gives an impatient huff. It is only once she has paid that it occurs to Johanna that half an hour has passed since she left Magda. What has she been doing talking to Father Christmases and staring at duty-free items? It's this place. It robs everything of its context. All she wants is to be with Magda. It's so strong, her desire to care for her, her need, her love, it's almost violent.

As Johanna pushes her way through the crowds back to Magda with the drink and the chocolate and the fluffy toy under her arm, she passes a band of girls in blue sweatshirts singing Christmas songs, along with a small frightened young lad in a turban. A group of onlookers has assembled to watch. Several people are dancing, including one of the Father Christmases and some more shop assistants dressed as angels.

'Aww, cute!' shout some of the singing girls on spotting Johanna.

She assumes they're referring to her lamb.

'We will have to put out a plea for help,' says Mrs Pike, chewing two Nicorettes, one at each side of her mouth.

She's forgotten the name of the girl with green hair again. She squints at her identity tag.

'Hester,' says the girl.

'I want you to ring the local radio station, Hester. Ask if anyone is looking to adopt a pet for Christmas.'

'There is another problem,' says Hester, twisting her hair. 'The donkey.'

'What about the donkey?'

'We are going to have to move her. She keeps trying to kick the cage with the cheetahs. It's upsetting them.'

'And where exactly are we going to put the donkey?'

'Maybe we could take her for a walk?' says Hester. 'It's not as if there are any planes taking off. Besides, it's getting awfully smelly out there.'

'You are suggesting we walk the donkey through the airport?'

Hester shrugs, as if to say she's seen worse. 'There's going to be a public-information announcement soon,' she adds. 'About what's going on.'

'Do you mean in the world generally,' asks Mrs Pike, 'or just inside my head?'

When the public-information announcement comes it is not very informative and not very public. It can only be heard in the duty-free shop and the women's toilets at the back of the departure lounge. It is also delivered by a woman who sounds as if she has clipped her nose with a peg and placed some sort of splint between her teeth.

'Due to un-chore-cheen chirchirmshtanches—'

Then she conks out.

'*What* did she say?' asks Mrs King.

And everyone around her in the duty-free shop repeats, 'What? What? *What?*'

Her daughters shrug. They are forty-two and forty-three respectively, both freshly single, and they are worse than teenagers. At least with teenagers, you know that spots and hormones and sulking are not permanent; but when they start all that at forty the outlook is less rosy. Why did Mrs King think it was a good idea to go on holiday with her daughters? She had been planning to get away from it all, the stress, the Christmas hoo-ha. Since the death of her husband a year ago, she has been finding it hard to do the simplest things. Every day she feels his absence, and as the seasons turn she says to herself, 'A year ago it was his birthday . . . A year ago it was our wedding anniversary . . . A year ago we went on holiday.' With the passing of each week, she feels a little more pulled away from her husband, a little more alone. Two of her oldest friends have died in the last few months; sometimes she feels she is looking out over a field that is becoming

95

thinner and thinner as she stands there. So she'd said to both Christina and Tracey on the phone, 'This year I want to get out of the country on Christmas Day.' She'd always had a thing about the Northern Lights, she'd told her daughters; in reality she was planning to close the front door and turn off the lights and sleep on and off until January. Only, would you believe it, her daughters must have picked up the phone to one another and discovered they, too, had a thing about the Northern Lights – a real thing, not a made-up one – and would be available to join her. She even had to pay for their tickets.

'Maybe we should go home,' says Mrs King. 'Maybe we should cut our losses.'

Christina glances up from her book. It is some sort of complicated guide to astrology. Her face is grim. And Tracey – who has bought herself an entire new snow outfit and is overheating by the second – says something she fails to hear. Mrs King is about to ask Tracey to repeat herself, but thinks better of it. Besides, she has other things to distract her. Fifteen buxom teenage girls in blue sweatshirts have just rushed into Duty-Free, followed by an exhausted-looking woman and a boy with a turban.

'Lambs!' croon the girls. 'Aww! Look at the ickle fluffy lambs! Miss! Miss! Can I get one, Miss?'

*

Johanna scans the waiting area but she can't find Magda anywhere. There is so much to see it is hard to keep remembering that all she is searching for is a plain young woman in a grey hoodie. The Father Christmases have found a group of children and are performing some sort of juggling act. A makeshift tent has been set up, offering hot drinks and (cold) toasted sandwiches for breakfast. You can barely move without treading on a sleeping body. Johanna tries to remember exactly where she left Magda, she tries to spot the man and woman in their linen travel suits, but she can't see anything she recognizes. She rings Magda's mobile phone. No answer.

She doesn't know whether to run, to walk, where to look. She has no idea how to do anything. She searches the women's toilets, the café, she scans the rows of seating, but there is no sign of Magda.

A boy begins to cry. 'I want my Buzz Lightyear outfit. I want it now!'

Johanna hears the boy's parents shouting and telling him he has to wait until Christmas, and then she hears the boy crying that it is Christmas, and his parents' confusing reply that yes, it is Christmas, but it is not *real* Christmas until they get on holiday. 'Why? Why?' cries the boy. 'Because, because,' they say. The boy's sobs hack straight through Johanna as if a part of her is crying too. And then, for the first time, the truth hits her and she reels. I am going to be a parent. I am going to share a child. A child who will want the impossible, whose needs will constantly bamboozle me, and who will cause me to say things I don't fully understand. I must find my partner. I must find Magda.

'But I don't need perfume,' says Mrs King.

'It's duty-free,' replies Christina. 'It's cheaper than in the shops. It can be your Christmas present.'

'Don't buy me a present,' says Mrs King. 'We agreed. No presents. If you buy me a present, I will have to buy one for you.'

'You haven't bought us a Christmas present?' gasps Tracey. She stumbles backwards like a snowy Michelin man.

Mrs King glances from one daughter to the other. They couldn't look less forgiving. 'But we *said* we wouldn't buy presents this year,' she says weakly.

'We didn't mean nothing *at all*,' says Christina. 'You're our mother. You're supposed to give us presents.'

'But you're grown-up,' says Mrs King, feeling her words lose confidence even as they leave her mouth.

'This is typical,' says Tracey. Despite her anger, her eyes fill with tears. She has to pretend she is blowing her nose.

'What is typical, Tracey?'

'Since Dad died, you only think of yourself.'

Now it is Mrs King who wants to stagger backwards, but she doesn't. She has noticed a change in her daughters. There was a time when they shared everything with their mother. Tracey would always ask for her advice about how to deal with problems at the school where she taught, and barely a day passed without Christina phoning, not to say anything in particular, just to check that her mother was still there, still listening. Mrs King used to hear the way her friends complained about their children, how difficult things were, and feel a touch of complacency. Even when the girls were teenagers, their mood swings had been short-lived. But since the death of their father, they've become formal, more removed. Spiteful, actually. As if it is their mother's fault they have no father. As if she could have done more to save him if only she'd made the effort.

'How about this for a plan?' she asks. 'We'll each choose our own gift.'

They emerge fifteen minutes later with perfume, a golden chocolate bar and a gift box of anti-ageing cream.

'Happy now?' asks Christina, and even the word 'happy' sounds like something she has trodden in.

*

Magda has to hold on to the sink in order to keep standing. She remains very still, hoping the pain won't find her again. She holds her breath.

'You can't stay here,' says a woman in a white overall. She holds a mop, but confusingly is also wearing a tinsel halo and a pair of large fluffy wings. 'These facilities are officially shut for cleaning purposes.'

'Can I lie down?' asks Magda. 'I don't feel very good.'

'You've got to be kidding,' says the angel. 'Have you looked at the state of the floor? If you're ill you need to report to the medical centre.'

'Where is the medical centre?'

'You have to ask at the information desk.'

But there is a queue for the information desk and there is so much noise, there are so many travellers shouting at the two officials (also dressed as angels but looking on the verge of tears) that Magda feels dizzy. She waits patiently in the queue, but the queue keeps spilling outwards and sideways as more people join it, all shouting questions at the angels. Instead she spots a floor plan and discovers that the medical centre is only at the other side of the departure lounge.

The pain is more frequent now, her stomach making a tight fist and growing rock hard. She has to walk very slowly, almost in and around the pain, as if it is lying in wait for her and one foot in the wrong place will set it off. The medical centre is locked. *Seasons Greetings!* says the sign.

Then she remembers Johanna – all she wants is Johanna – and with that thought comes the realization that she has lost her bag. She must make her way back to where she was waiting before, only she can't think where that was because it all looks the same. Her breathing is fast and high in her chest. She has to go very slowly because she is about to drop something, she can't carry it any more. She has never felt so alone. People push past, not noticing her distress. Someone even jabs her in the stomach with a rucksack.

An arm shoots out and pulls her close and Magda is about to fight it off until she realizes it is Johanna's.

'You look awful. What's happening?'

'I don't know,' she moans. 'I don't know.'

'Do you need a doctor?'

'There isn't one.'

'We need to get you away from all these people.'

But it's too late. Water – a tide of water is rising. Magda had no idea there could be so much of it. She can't move. She can't even get back to the toilets. She experiences a pressure mounting inside her and then a kind of pop. Her legs are wet, as if someone has thrown a bucket of warm water at her.

'Oh my God,' says Johanna, noticing Magda's jogging pants.

Magda moans. 'It's happening.'

'Now? Here? It can't—'

Magda's neck flips backwards as a new wave of contractions passes through her. Her eyes are closed and her skin is clammy and grey. She grips her fingers tightly around Johanna's arm as if she is afraid of being pulled away by the pain.

'I'll ring for an ambulance,' shouts Johanna. And then she remembers the gridlocked traffic surrounding the airport. How will an ambulance get through?

'It's too late,' moans Magda again. 'No.' The 'no' becomes more of a low, like a cow groaning. Magda rocks from one foot to the other, trying to contain the pain. Johanna forgets all about the ambulance. People are beginning to turn and look. 'I can't walk any more. Jo, I am going to have our baby here. Find a trolley. Get me somewhere quiet.'

'I can't leave you. I'll carry you.' Johanna tries to put her arms around Magda, but Magda shrieks as if her touch is a vice around her stomach. Several more people turn to look.

Magda whispers through clenched teeth, 'I'll be OK. I'll wait. I won't move from here. I promise.'

'You're sure?'

'Yes. It's OK so long as I don't walk. Find me a trolley.'

There is no sign of anyone in the departure lounge who looks vaguely official, let alone a person with a trolley. Maybe the staff are all involved in trying to sort out the unforeseen circumstances. Or maybe they are in hiding, afraid that if they go out and try to explain the situation they will be torn apart with questions and complaints. The only staff to be seen are the two at the information desk dressed as Christmas angels, as if to say, *No, no, don't ask us for help, we are only jokes!* The six Father Christmases are now disco-dancing as the Stroud Girls' Choir performs its entire Christmas medley.

Johanna asks the girl in Duty-Free, and the angel-woman cleaning the toilets; she asks families, women who look like mothers and should surely understand, but no one can offer her a trolley on which to transport Magda somewhere more private.

She spots a small building at the other side of the concourse. Before anyone can stop her, Johanna blunders through a door clearly marked *No Entry* and finds herself outside. The door slams behind her.

'Apparently a little girl has rung. About the goat.'

'The what?' says Mrs Pike. She is trying to work out where to put the donkey. She has taken it for a walk around the concourse, and now that she wants to put it back inside its cage it keeps baring its teeth. It is definitely upsetting the four cheetahs. They whip round and round their cage, snarling.

'The goat.'

'Oh, that,' says Mrs Pike.

'The little girl says she wants to adopt it. But not the terrapin. Her mum has a van. Also there's a woman in reception. She's looking for a stretcher. Her wife is having a baby.'

Mrs Pike gives a laugh that verges on the deranged.

Tracey and Christina King pass the time discussing other travellers. It's a game they always used to play when they were children. Questions like: Where do you think that family is going? Then they move on to other stories. 'There's this kid at school,' says Tracey. 'He wants to be a girl . . .'

'What's that?' asks Mrs King, passing her daughters the sandwiches she has queued for and also the free bottled water.

On noticing her mother, Tracey appears to clam up. 'Nothing,' she says. Christina opens the packaging on her sandwich. Her nails are pale-blue talons.

Sometimes Mrs King feels she is searching for something without even knowing what it is. Something that will put things back together with her daughters. She wonders if she'll ever find it, whether the search will always hurt the way it does, not exactly painful but always there, like an ache in a joint that comes with age. A miracle. That is what she is looking for. Never mind the Northern Lights.

'What's going on over there?' says Tracey, pointing to the other side of the departure lounge.

Johanna puts her arms around Magda and walks her slowly through the crowds. 'You're just going to have to let me help,' she whispers. 'I know this isn't how we planned it.'

Magda grips Johanna's hand but she can't do words any more, only guttural sounds that are more like animal cries. She wants to say it doesn't hurt, not in the sense of pain that comes from the outside, but the baby gives a kick, a really hard one, as if it is thinking of booting its way out through her belly, and she stops still, her shoulders hunched, her face creased, her hands gripped into tight balls.

'Not far, not far,' murmurs Johanna. She wipes the slick of sweat from Magda's forehead and kisses her hand.

Magda closes her eyes as the pain punches through her.

When she opens them, she sees a girl with green hair and an older woman, frantically chewing.

'Don't be frightened,' calls Johanna.

Then the voices become distant unconnected noise, like a sound beyond a window. Magda feels the clasp of firm hands beneath her armpits and others taking hold of her legs. Her feet are no longer on the ground. Her face rests on something soft and warm that smells of sweet dung and hay.

She moves forward and it is like swinging.

'Miss!' interrupts one of the Stroud Girls' Choir, clutching her fluffy lamb. 'There's a woman on a donkey.'

'Don't be so ridiculous,' says Shelley.

It is Hester's idea that they fetch blankets.

'Why will we need blankets?' asks Mrs Pike.

'For the blood,' says Hester. 'You hold on to the donkey and I will fetch blankets.'

Mrs Pike has given birth three times herself and has been present at the births of two of her grandchildren, but she has never seen it happen so fast. One minute the girl is on the donkey and making her way towards the animal reception centre, led by Mrs Pike, the next she is yelling, 'This is it! It's happening right here!' The women drag her down from the donkey and she crawls on her hands and knees towards the ladies' toilets at the back of the departure lounge, gasping and groaning. Someone shouts about fetching a doctor, calling an ambulance, but the girl shakes her head; it's too late. Mrs Pike follows and hears a soft braying and remembers she is still leading the donkey. An angel with a mop says, 'You can't come in here, these facilities are closed for cleaning,' and Mrs Pike says, 'Are you kidding? You're going to need a lot more than a mop in a minute.' She wedges the door open and the pregnant girl crawls towards the sinks.

The girl screams for the other woman, the one who is like a painted blue fish with pink hair, and grips hold of her hand. Someone has the kindness to throw a coat over the girl and Mrs Pike shoves the donkey reins into the hands of the angel so that she can help the girl pull off her clothes.

Hester returns, carrying bundles of blankets, towels, scissors, cotton balls, a bottle of disinfectant and a small cardboard carton. 'I couldn't leave the terrapin,' she says. And instead of asking, 'Why? Why couldn't you leave the terrapin?' Mrs Pike nods and accepts that babies are born on Christmas Day at the airport whilst young women with green hair rescue small illegal reptiles and stow them in boxes. The women take the blankets and tuck them around the pregnant girl as she writhes and pushes with the pain. Her legs are shaking so hard they are flapping against the floor. Her thin pale face shines through a film of sweat.

'Can someone close the door?' calls Mrs Pike. 'Let's give this girl more privacy.' People are beginning to gather outside.

The angel says she can't close the door, on account of the donkey.

'There, there,' says Hester, grabbing the free hand of the pregnant girl. 'I've got my sister on my phone. She's a nurse. She's gonna tell me how to help and we are gonna deliver this baby of yours. All right?'

'Yes,' moans Magda.

'Yes,' moans Johanna.

'My sister says I gotta take a look down there. Is that all right?' She dips her head beneath the coat and shrieks. 'Oh my God, I can see a fucking head. Everybody wash your hands. Quick! Breathe, darlin'. My sister says you gotta breathe!'

Magda is aware of Johanna's voice telling her to breathe. She is being ripped open, but she must breathe.

'Can you hear me?' says some green hair.

Magda nods to show she can.

'My sister says you gotta focus on one thing,' says the green hair. 'OK? Can you do that? 'Cos in a second I'm gonna ask you to give a really big push. And don't forget those big deep breaths. That's my girl.'

'Breathe!' shout Mrs Pike and the angel in unison.

'Ooof!' Johanna gives a huge expulsion of air. She looks ready to pass out.

Magda opens her eyes. All around her she sees a blur of women's faces. But beyond them something catches her attention, a stab of red. It is the advert with the young woman in the snow. And so Magda thinks of the girl out there, like the deer she once saw, all alone and not knowing what will happen next. As the pain comes and goes, the red coat swells in and out of focus, as if the two things have joined up in time. She hears the young woman with her red coat call her name: *Magda! Magda! You can do this, Magda!* She hears other voices, girls' voices, laughter, and carol-singing, and she doesn't know any more if it is the red coat or the people around her, or something altogether more ancient. Ghosts from another time. The young woman with her red coat steps into Magda's imagination and Magda follows her through snow. As something pushes its way through her body and between her legs, Magda hears the calls from the friends the girl has left behind, she sees torches, she smells the flinty coldness of snow, the way it pads the world in stillness.

'Push!' yells the green hair. And *Push!* shouts the girl in her red coat. 'PUSH!' choruses the assembled crowd.

'It's coming! It's coming!' someone shouts.

'Our baby,' cries Johanna.

'Oh my God,' sobs the green hair. 'It's a girl!'

'Due to un-chore-cheen chirchirmshtanches,' announces the public announcement. And then she splutters to another halt.

A baby? A birth in the departure lounge? Yes, people are saying. A baby. But where? Where?

Fifteen singing choir girls clutching duty-free lambs fly past Mrs King and her daughters. They are followed by the same tired-looking woman Mrs King saw earlier and the boy with his head in a turban. They in turn are followed by airport staff dressed as angels and six Father Christmases.

'Which is the way to the new baby?' calls Mrs King.

'Hallelujah,' sing the girls. 'Follow a star . . .'

A dull light leaks from the sky. The day is like any other, so weak it has no colour. But there is no freak weather. No snow storm. There is just a mass of cloud between the earth and the firmament that hangs flat and still. Then an easterly wind picks up, whipping the cloud, sending it scurrying and boiling, until a hole is ripped right through its centre and, without warning, sunlight pours down in a thick, flowing golden shaft. It's as though someone has just hit a giant flash bulb. In an instant, everything inside the airport is illuminated, caught in this tremor of pure sunlight. The light lands inside the opened door of the ladies' toilets. It shines.

There is Magda with her baby, and Johanna; Shelley, Winston and the Stroud Girls' Choir with their lambs; Mrs Pike and the donkey, Hester and her terrapin; Mrs King and her daughters bearing bags from Duty-Free, along with six Father Christmases, shop assistants dressed as angels, several women from Security and a band of air hostesses who have heard the news and come to investigate. All around them the air shimmers in a shower of dust.

'Wait for me!' calls a little boy, running to join the scene. He is dressed in some sort of space-hero suit.

'Who's that?' asks Mrs Pike.

'Oh, he's Buzz Lightyear,' replies Hester, scooping up towels. For the first time all morning the two women seem to pause and see each other.

'Merry Christmas, Hester,' says Mrs Pike.

The sky is streaked with bands of orange and gold and flaming red. Then, just as suddenly as the light came, a low nimbostratus cloud moves in and everything is grey once more.

Already there are announcements that the technical problems have been resolved; all flights will be resumed; please report to Check-in. Men with clipboards and walkie-talkies have begun to appear, as well as a doctor, several policemen and a team from Immigration.

Mrs King holds out her arms and pulls her daughters close. At moments such as these we understand instinctively what it means to exist. It doesn't matter where a birth happens, she thinks – in a stable, in an airport, or even in the more conventional settings, such as the maternity ward at the hospital – it is a miracle each time. And there are other miracles, too, that take place throughout every human life: when a child takes those first steps and does not fall, or when we realize our children are steady now and we let go.

'Girls,' whispers Mrs King. 'Shall we . . . ?'

She has said all that she needs to say. The three Kings place their gifts at the feet of the mother and her newborn child.

The Boxing Day Ball

It was too muddy to cross the fields and the girls hadn't a car between them. They had no choice but to make their way along the lanes, though it would add almost an hour to the journey. The land shone icy blue in the moonlight as if the colour had been chilled out of it. Sometimes the girls saw a light in the distance, but mostly it was just dark and cold.

There were ten girls, including the twins, and they moved in a weaving column of ones and twos. A few carried paraffin lamps. Patty Driscoll had a torch. Now and then someone would holler out a song to keep the rhythm going, something like the Christmas number one that year, 'Return To Sender!', and the others would pitch in with the chorus. Their breath hung in front of them. They carried their dance shoes in bags and gripped their collars to their throats.

Maureen kept to the back in her short red coat. Her fingers stung with the loneliness of the cold and so did her feet, but it was not a sad loneliness. There was something in the air. She could feel it.

'Ain't we there yet?' That was Patty Driscoll.

'Not yet,' shouted Esther Hughes. Like Patty, she spoke without sounding her *t*s. Maureen had lived in the village all her life and she still couldn't get the accent. No matter how hard she tried, she still sounded like a stranger.

'Si-i-lent night,' sang the girls until one of them shouted, 'Blinkin'-cold night,' and they sang that instead.

It was cold, all right. 1962 was the worst winter anyone could remember. Clouds were no more than single ribbons beneath the silver-gleaming halo of the moon and stars were shot points in the sky. Sheep stood pale as stones in the fields and birds sat pegged on the black branches of the trees. Everything was apart and waiting, as still as a held breath. Maureen imagined mice, half-frozen, poked down underground holes; there would be rats, voles, shrews, worms, spiders, rabbits and badgers. Foxes, even. Just beneath her feet. Right where she couldn't see. All poised, all waiting.

Patty Driscoll shouted it 'ud half-kill her, the blinkin' walking, and Maureen smiled, but only to herself, because even if she was like a stranger she knew you didn't laugh at Patty Driscoll. She felt a swell of love for them all that night, even Patty. The factory girls had watched her every

116

morning on her way to school. She had not been allowed to mix with them, not even as a child, though she knew some of them by sight – the twins, for instance, along with Esther, because the twins went everywhere hand in hand and Esther was so pale and elongated, almost starved-looking, you couldn't forget her. Patty Driscoll, too; she was another one you wouldn't forget, always with a beaten-up look. Maureen had sensed their eyes raking her up and down as she passed their bus stop in the mornings and she had shrunk inside her coat. Then one morning they had called, 'Hey, you!', and asked if she wanted a ticket for the Boxing Day Ball. She had assumed it was a joke. She had assumed they were laughing at her.

'Everyone goes,' one of the twins had said. 'It's the best night of the year.'

'No,' she had told them. 'No, thank you.' But once the idea was in her head she had not been able to get rid of it. Her parents would not approve. 'I think not,' her mother would say; 'I think not.' When the girls called out and asked her again, a week later, she had said yes. Yes, she would like a ticket. The words were out of her mouth before her head could stop them.

'Thass it, then,' they had said. 'We'll go together, Maureen.' So they knew her name. They were not laughing at her, after all.

She had kept the ticket hidden in her coat pocket. She would not go. Girls like Maureen did not go to the Boxing Day Ball.

And now here it was again. That little throb of excitement, as if something were about to change. Maybe it was the nip of gin Esther Hughes had offered from a bottle at the start. Maureen had not tasted gin before and she could feel the sting of it still, like a hot hole at the back of her throat. Then a sudden wind lifted the girls' coats like a dirty old man and they all shrieked, 'Aghh, get off, will ya!'

'My hair will be a blinkin' mess by the time we get there,' said Patty Driscoll. This time it was safe to laugh because Patty was shining her torch to her face and squishing up her mouth, showing a bruise under her left eye like a purple flower. She was right about her hair, though. It had sprung from its clips and fizzed out in a copper mane. Some of the girls had fixed their curls with tape. Esther Hughes wore her rollers pinned to her scalp under a scarf. She was going to leave them to the last minute. She had Elnett hairspray in her handbag and also a bottle of that Black Rose perfume. She got it for Christmas, she said.

'You don't wanna know what I got for Christmas,' said Patty Driscoll.

Maureen had received a book about deportment and a set of silver-backed hairbrushes. She had eaten Christmas lunch with her parents in the chill of the dining room, none of them speaking, wearing paper hats like crowns. Afterwards her mother had washed and put away the china tureens and best glasses, as if she were tidying away Christmas, and her father had taken his nap in front of the fire. She wanted to grab hold of her childhood home – the matching curtains, the cross-stitched tea towels, the embroidered covers for armchairs in case of stains, the needlework samplers that said *A Woman's Work is Never Done* and *One is Nearer God's Heart in the Garden than Anywhere Else on Earth* – and ditch the lot. Instead she had fetched the ball ticket from her coat pocket.

'What is that?' her mother had asked.

'You should put your hair up,' said one of the girls. It took Maureen a moment to realize the girl was talking to her. Her name was Charleen Williams. That was it. There were so many to remember. Her father had been a GI in the war.

'I am not very good at doing my hair,' said Maureen. She could feel herself blush. Her hair was dark and very fine and it never seemed to do anything except hang on either side of her head.

'You'd look like that film star. Whass her name?'

'Audrey Hepburm,' piped up Patty Driscoll.

'Thass the one. You shoulda let me do your hair. Wanna ciggie, Maureen?'

'No, thank you.' Maureen did not smoke. She hadn't even tried.

'Give us a ciggie!' squawked Esther Hughes, and so did Patty Driscoll.

'I only got one packet,' complained Charleen, but she offered them around and struck matches between the girls' cupped hands and their faces were briefly illuminated like ghosts in the dark. 'So why do you still go to school, Maureen?'

She said, 'I am going to secretarial college.' That sounded better than university.

'Maureen's clever, see,' laughed one of the twins, either Pauline or Paulette Gordon, it was impossible to tell which because they wore matching coats and boots and hair ribbons. 'She's got more brains than the rest of us put together.'

'Better get a move on,' said Esther, checking her hair rollers and stepping forward. Someone began to yell 'Ding dong merrily on high' and they all sang along. When they got to the high notes of 'Gloria' they cackled and screeched like witches.

The Boxing Day Ball took place every winter. Maureen

knew that much. People came from miles around. All sorts of people, not just the factory workers and the farm hands, but also the university boys home for Christmas, and even the young professionals if they weren't yet attached. Charleen said she was going to land herself a nice office lad this year. She was fed up with them good-for-nothing tinkers and farm boys.

The only parties that Maureen had attended were those of her mother's friends. She had met their sons, all stiff partings and knitted pullovers, and she had tried on more than one occasion to fall in love, as required, over Viennese fingers and pots of tea. The women spoke about their husbands, what they did for a living, and Maureen's mother would go quiet, studying her hands, because her husband had retired early on account of his heart. He hadn't even gone to war like the rest of the men, he had worked in the munitions factory, although Maureen's mother referred to it as undercover work. The war had been twenty years ago, but people still talked about it. 'Do try to look interested,' her mother would whisper. 'I *am* trying to look interested,' Maureen would answer. Her mother would draw up her chest as if she intended to self-inflate and say, 'You are yawning.' And when Maureen replied that she only wanted to laugh, was that too much? her mother would lift her eyebrows and say, 'I think not. I think not.'

121

Maureen would never be like her mother. When the chance came, she would say 'I think so' to everything.

Out of the darkness, lights began to emerge. The girls passed close-together cottages with lit-up windows and Christmas trees. Esther Hughes said she wanted to stop and look; she'd never had a tree in her house 'cos her brothers would only knock it over and shred her mother's nerves. The pinched hardness melted from Esther's face as she took in the shining baubles, the silver tinsel, the Christmas angel perched at the top, until she looked like a child. Then the other girls crowded next to her, smiling and cooing 'Ahhh!' and Maureen could see the child in them too.

She thought of those people inside their houses, watching television if they had a set, or making sandwiches with leftover turkey. She imagined her father dozing at home in the armchair, her mother stabbing a cross-stitch tapestry with her needle, and she was glad she was out here, in the cold night. The wind had dropped again and the air smelt flinty. Roof tiles shone like blue fish scales.

'Thass it, look!' shouted Patty Driscoll.

Far ahead Maureen could make out the faint yellowy glow of the hall, and a dotting of smaller lights twining through the dark. She took a deep breath to steady herself.

She fancied she could hear the faraway thump of music and it was like a part of her, like the beat of her heart.

She followed the girls.

'You are not going to the Boxing Day Ball,' her mother had said, 'and that's final.' But Maureen had stood her ground. 'I'm eighteen now,' she'd said. 'You can't stop me.' She could not look her mother in the eye. Had she asked her father's permission? Of course not. He was a gentle man, softly spoken, always apologizing for not being well, always saying he was a burden until it got tiring to keep saying, 'No, no, you're not.' 'How do you think it is for me?' her mother had asked. And Maureen had shrugged uncomfortably because the question seemed to come from a part of her mother she had not met before. 'Don't say I didn't warn you,' said her mother, turning on her heels and leaving the room.

The dance was already underway. A queue spilled from the door and several boys loitered in stiff jackets that were either too big or too small, smoking cigarettes between pinched fingers. Patty Driscoll and Esther Hughes shifted impatiently, trying to get a better view of the young men who would later partner them, trying to get a first picture of the hall. A shadowy couple was already up against the wall. 'That Judith Hoggs, Christ, she ain't got no shame,' said one of the girls. Another boy was on his stomach, half under the bushes.

Esther said, 'Thass Peter Green. He ain't having a good time unless he's spewing up his insides.'

The girls stopped and cheered. 'Go on, Peter. Spill it out, boy!'

It was no wonder Maureen's mother had never been to a Boxing Day Ball.

The doorman was dressed as Father Christmas. He wore a red velour hat and a fake white beard along with a red jacket that didn't quite button over the swell of his stomach. Holding each ticket up to the light, he examined it as if he suspected forgery, so that even though Maureen had paid for her ticket, she felt nervous. Once he was satisfied that the ticket was a real one, he took an ink stamp and made a blue mark on the back of Maureen's hand. 'Ho, ho, ho,' he said to the girls, catching their fingers.

'Have we been a good girl?' he asked Patty Driscoll's breasts.

'Oh fuck off, Santa,' she said, pushing past.

Inside the hall Patty shucked off her mackintosh and handed it to the woman in charge of the cloakroom. Maureen unbuttoned her red coat and did the same. The other girls wore mini skirts and short frocks and they tugged at their hems and shoulder straps. 'You are not going dressed like that,' her mother had said, entering the bedroom while Maureen got ready. Maureen had been confused; she always wore her white blouse and plaid skirt. Her mother left the room as quietly as she had entered and returned with a black satin dress. 'Try this.' The dress had a sweetheart neckline with a nipped waist and fitted skirt. Maureen had never seen it before, though she could tell from the neatness of the stitching that her mother had made it. She could tell, too, that it had never been worn. And all the time that Maureen's mother had helped her into the dress and fastened the zip and led her to the mirror, she had said nothing. She had only worn that tightened look that made Maureen feel both a burden and desperate to be free. 'Does this mean you are letting me go?' Maureen had asked. In reply her mother had said, 'I'll wave from upstairs. No need to call out. No need to wake your father.'

The parish hall was a big building with a polished wooden floor. The bare light bulbs had been replaced with more festive red ones and they hung the length of the dance floor like giant red berries. There were homemade evergreen banners and coloured paper chains strung between the metal rafters. A ball of mistletoe had been hung at the centre and the young people avoided passing beneath it as if it were dangerous. Tables were arranged along the walls, covered with paper cloths and sprigs of ivy. At the far end there was a makeshift stage, also decorated with evergreens and a small decorated Christmas tree, where a DJ was playing records. Behind him the band were already unpacking their instruments. They did it slowly, tuning their guitars, setting up the drums, trying to look nonchalant. They wore suits and two-tone shirts and the singer had a necklace like a giant gold ball of sun.

The hall was already full, though only a few people stood up near the stage. Instead they hovered as if they hadn't quite decided whether they were going to dance or just stand there, having a look. Most people were gathered in groups close to the walls – the farm boys in what looked like borrowed jackets, the young men in full dinner suits and bow ties. Groups of girls clustered around the tables. When they greeted one another or picked up their drinks, when they offered their laps as seats, and even when they laughed, they did it with exaggeration and a sideways glance to check who might be watching. Maureen recognized a boy with oiled hair from one of her mother's friends' parties. She thought the young man was called Howard. If he wasn't, he ought to be. She looked away before he could spot her. The floor beneath the mistletoe ball lay empty and polished, like still water.

The caller took his place at the front of the stage. And now here came the girls, stepping into line on one side of the hall, giggling with their friends, offering embarrassed half-glances across the dance floor, making a fuss about swapping places. Here came the boys, slowly, checking their ties, some of them still holding their drinks, with a look of studied casualness as if it were quite by chance that they, too, were falling into line. Charleen stood opposite the boy Maureen recognized and she gave a wonky grimace. Patty didn't seem to have a partner. Esther's curled hair was already flat. Pauline and Paulette Gordon were hand in hand. The band started up. The couples stepped forward.

And away they went, hands crossed, galloping the length of the floor, up one way and back the other, down the middle and along the sides, joining hands as they met again, some of them slapping into the walls, the top couple gripping damp hands to form an arch, the others hurtling beneath. One dance after another with only brief intervals to buy drinks from the bar. Left arms linked to move in a circle, then back to back, then casting off to dance outside the set. Cross hands, counter clockwise, figure of eight, up a double and back. Maureen could feel the pounding of their feet through the floor and it was as though the hall itself was dancing.

'Ain't you got no partner, Maureen?' shouted Patty Driscoll. After over an hour of dancing, her face was red as a cherry. She was so breathless she could barely get her words out.

Maureen shook her head. She had stood on the side for a while and she had joined in for a while, but now she was watching someone so hard she could not really see anyone else.

She had noticed him from the start. She couldn't miss him. Whilst the other couples danced in groups and pairs, he jived by himself in the middle of the dance floor. Sometimes they bumped straight into him, sometimes they caught him in a circle, but he didn't seem to notice or care. Arms out, head shaking, legs kicking; the flaps of his coat flew like dog-tooth-check sails. It was as if he was dancing out something that was inside him. He looked wild. Half insane. But he looked free. She'd never seen anything like it.

'Who's that?' Maureen asked.

'We call him No-Mum,' said Patty Driscoll.

'Why do you call him No-Mum?' During the conversation, she'd lost him again, the wild-dancing young man. She was afraid he'd already gone.

' 'Cos he's got no mum.'

'Where is his mum?'

'She left. And his dad's a right bastard.' Patty closed her eyes and staggered a little, losing her balance. 'I love the ball. I don't ever want to go home.' She galloped back to the dance floor and Maureen shifted to one side for a better view.

There he was, the boy, still dancing alone. He was like a stranger in the room, a person from a foreign place who did not understand how things were supposed to be done. She kept watching and she was aware of time passing and she smiled. So long as she could keep him in her eye line, that was enough.

Maybe he sensed her watching because he stopped suddenly and looked back at her. Then he danced some more, for another half-hour or so, and she continued watching, but it was different now because he surely knew she was watching. He did not stop and neither did she look away. It was the raw energy of him that moved her. The completeness of what he was. He stopped again. Caught her eye again. Then he threaded his way through the crowd and stopped so close she could feel the heat of his skin. He smelt sweet, like oranges.

He stooped with his mouth pointed towards her ear and lifted a small lock of her hair so that he could speak to her and be heard. The boldness of the gesture sent prickles of electricity shooting down the length of her neck. Maureen held her breath as if to stop time.

His voice touched her ear, surprisingly soft and close. It was as though he had actually slipped inside her head and was speaking to her from her bones. 'You could always be my wife,' he said.

Did he? Did he say that? He moved aside and gazed down at her, waiting for her reply, his face serious to show that whatever it was he had just said, he meant it. Or was it, 'You could always give me a light'? Was that what he had said?

She studied his face, searching for clues, and all she could see was the deep blue of his eyes. He did not stop gazing down at her. Clearly he needed his answer. In her embarrassment she felt her skin stain with heat, and before she could do anything about it a cry of laughter shot from her mouth. It wasn't funny, it wasn't at all funny, but now that she had started, she really couldn't stop. And all the time she laughed, he watched, a smile quirking the corners of his mouth, as though he were both intrigued and delighted that he had done this, that he had made her laugh so suddenly and uncontrollably. She had no idea if he had asked her to marry him or had asked for a light, and so she said the first thing that came into her head.

'You'd better buy me a drink first.'

She had never said that to a boy before. It was the

sort of thing Patty Driscoll and the other girls would say.

Now it was the boy's turn to laugh, and as he did, little tucks and creases flew from his eyes towards his cheeks. Then he shrugged his shoulders and walked away.

She watched him waiting his turn at the bar. He didn't look back and it gave her a proper opportunity to take in his height, his hair combed into a quiff, his coat that stopped short of his wrists and knees and was too small. Perhaps it wasn't even his. She had never seen anyone so complete and so alone, and it made her laugh just to keep watching. Then the woman behind the bar must have asked what he wanted because she nodded and went to fetch his order. The woman laughed when she came back to him with two drinks. It seemed to be an effect he had.

He pushed his way towards Maureen, holding out two plastic cups. When he saw her waiting, she could tell he was moved, that he had believed she would go and was both relieved and touched that he was wrong. He smiled in a shy way, as if he couldn't quite face her, and she smiled too to show him not to be afraid. They touched their plastic cups carefully. The drink was clear; she guessed it must be gin. She didn't want gin but she wanted to accept his kindness so she took a gulp of breath and stopped her nose. She decided to empty the cup in one go and get it over and done with.

It was tap water.

Maureen smiled, more deeply this time, as if she knew the boy and he knew her. 'Thank you,' she said, projecting her voice clearly above the music so that he could be in no doubt.

'That's OK.' He lifted his cup to his mouth and knocked it back. Afterwards he wiped his mouth with the side of his hand. 'What's your name?'

'Maureen.'

'Maureen.' He said it again, 'Maureen,' as if he were trying to get the taste of the word. Maureen had a feeling that he wanted to stay and tell her something else and she wanted the same, and yet there was nothing else to say and so they looked at the dance floor.

In the far corner Maybe-Howard was approaching a girl in coral. He gave a little bow as he offered his hand and then he turned the colour of her dress while he waited for her to answer. She shook her head but the girls around her pushed her forward so that she landed against him, then he in turn pushed her away as if overwhelmed.

It was almost the end of the evening. Maureen had no idea how it had passed so quickly. The singer left the stage and the band began to play 'Auld Lang Syne', and once again the floor began to fill. Maybe-Howard and the coral-dress girl were shuffling in a stiff wooden circle, her

132

hands perched like claws on his shoulders. Pauline and Paulette Gordon swayed in a threesome with Peter Green. Patty Driscoll was slow-dancing with Esther Hughes, her chin heavy on Esther's bone-thin shoulder, the halo of her orange hair touching Esther's lips, her large hands around Esther's scrawny fingers. And there was the singer, his mouth open wide over Charleen's, as if he were emptying every song he knew straight inside her.

Maureen watched them all. This was how it was, she thought. People would find one another, and sometimes it would last moments and sometimes it would last years. You could spend your life with a person and not understand them and then you could meet a boy across a dance floor and feel you knew him like a part of yourself. Maybe it was the same out there in the fields. Maybe the sheep were sitting two by two with the foxes and so were the rats and worms.

She thought of her mother, the way she had gazed out from the upstairs window as Maureen walked away, not waving or smiling, as if willing her daughter not to come back.

'You look in a world of your own,' said the boy.

She smiled. 'I was.'

'They were saying at the bar there's snow.'

'There can't be.'

133

'I know,' he said. 'Still. That's what they're saying. So you and I could stay here, wondering about it. Or we could go outside and look.'

Without another word he turned his back on her and moved towards the door. This time she followed. She did not think. He reached his hand backwards as if, even without looking, he knew she would be there. His fingers curled in a perfect fit around hers.

And if anyone had said to her that night as they made their way past the embracing couples, across the parish hall with the floor all sticky now, the evergreen garlands unhooked and hanging like limbs, the paper chains in torn-up fragments on the dancers' shoulders, if anyone had said that this was the man she would soon marry, abandoning all thought of university, that they would share a child and one day lose him, that they would move into separate bedrooms and talk over breakfast about nothing because silence, or something close to it, would be easier than words, that they would forget the Boxing Day Ball and the things that had seemed so funny, she would have hung her head so that her long hair lapped her cheeks. 'No, no,' she would have said, and then perhaps, 'I think—'

But this was all to come. For now, the boy helped her into her red coat and pulled open the door. The sting of the cold almost pushed her backwards.

'Well, look at that.' He laughed.

The moon was gone, the land an even paler blue. All around them swirled the Boxing Day snow, like melting stars. It seemed to be both lifting out of the ground and tipping from the sky. Her life was her own. It wasn't her mother's and it wasn't Patty Driscoll's or any of those other girls'. She thought of the boy dancing, the question he had posted into her ear. The answer was so simple, so clear, there was nothing to do but laugh, as if to laugh and feel happiness was the most serious thing in the world. Almost unbearable.

She said, 'Yes.'

'Yes?'

'Yes.' She did not turn her head to face him. She did not need to. She would see him now, everywhere she looked. He would be a part of everything and she did not even know his name. It was no less than a small miracle.

She stood in silence and looked up at the falling snow.

A Snow Garden

The boys kept asking if there would be snow at the new flat. 'Yes,' he told them. It began as a joke but then it got serious. 'Yes, Yes, YES!' 'I don't know why you keep promising there will be snow,' his sister said when she rang. 'It only happens in films and that bloody advert.' 'Because it's what everyone wants,' Henry told her. 'They want snow. It's traditional. It makes Christmas – you know.'

'What exactly?'

'Magical,' he said, but with a rising inflection so that instead of sounding certain he only sounded sort of desperate.

'Are you sure you're ready for this?' his sister asked. 'You can't afford to blow it, Henry.'

She was right. As always. There was so much to fix before the boys arrived. Henry checked every day but she was right about the weather too; there was no snow forecast. There was no forecast for anything much except low-level grey cloud. Sometimes the day had barely got going before it turned dark again.

Meanwhile Henry's head was feverish, flurrying with all the details he had to get sorted. First off, the flat needed a lick of paint. Henry had bought the place ten months ago just after the divorce came through and so far he had taken no interest in it whatsoever. The flat – not even *his* flat, but *the* flat, as if it was a neutral space he'd drifted into and might leave at any moment, the middle of the night maybe, whenever the urge took him – the flat was somewhere Henry ate a takeaway after work and drank a glass of milk whilst watching television until his eyes burnt so hard they had no choice but to close. When he washed a mug or a plate he replaced it not in a cupboard but in its storage box. Sometimes he even re-wrapped it in newspaper; he found his belongings seemed super-imposed on his life and had nothing to do with him. Even his sons didn't quite seem to fit. At the weekends Henry went to the park or he drove to his sister for a proper Sunday roast. Bea was five years younger than Henry but behaved like his mother. Well, someone had to, she often joked.

'I wish I wasn't going away,' she said.

'I'll manage. It's OK.'

'I don't even like skiing.' They laughed. And then she

asked, 'So what will you do with the boys? Six days is a long time.'

'Oh, I have lots planned.'

'You do?' He could hear the surprise in her voice and also relief. She was trying not to show it and this made him sad, for some reason.

'Well, bye now. I must get on with things,' he said.

Normally when Henry had an arrangement to see the boys it was only for the afternoon. He never met them at the old family house because he still couldn't face going back; it made him feel too guilty and uncomfortable. He'd allow a few hours for the drive down the motorway, stopping at a service station for coffee, and there he'd plan all the things he might do with the boys, though when it came to it he always did the same thing and took them to the pictures. It was easier to watch a film than sit around a table, just the three of them, not knowing what to say. It was certainly easier than something like a museum. ('And who even goes to museums?' asked Conor. His older son had become so ashen and elongated it looked as if his height was robbing him of both colour and ballast. Feathery hints of a beard shadowed his jawline and upper lip; his face had a hard, unforgiving look. 'I might like to go to a museum,' said Owen. Unlike his fifteen-year-old brother, Owen had not grown at all.) After the film, there

141

was always just enough time to eat. Sometimes Henry suggested Chinese food, but to his relief they always chose stuffed-crust pizzas, which they ate from the boxes in Henry's car. There was something about the packaging and the car that kept everything small and temporary and eyes-down, where it was easiest. If Henry braved a question about school or home or Debbie, the boys said, 'Fine.' Everything was 'fine'. No more, no less. It was like meeting an unfamiliar wall where there had once been plain, open spaces. Henry still couldn't get the hang of it.

But there had been a shift. 'An advancement,' his sister called it. Now that Henry had landed a new job and settled into the flat, the boys were going to stay with him from 27 December to 1 January. It would be the longest period Henry had spent with his sons since his breakdown and the divorce. 'Your looney tune,' as his ex-wife Debbie referred to it, saying 'toon' to rhyme with 'loon'.

Henry bought a tin of blue paint for the bedroom. He chose a cheap pine bunk bed in the sales with a matching set of drawers. He bought a set of matching plates and glasses with stems and a full set of cutlery. He tried to find a picture so that the flat would appear more lived-in and chose a reduced-price winter scene in a plastic clip-on frame because it looked seasonal, the trees piled with white, the deep troughs of snow, the young woman in her red coat and all those cartoon animals. The snow picture made Henry feel calm, as if a hand was resting on his shoulders and a soft voice was telling him to sleep. It was a long time since he'd felt like that. Often he sat looking at the picture, not thinking anything really, only looking. The young woman seemed happy but a part of him still felt sorry for her. He wondered what happened next in her story, because there must be a next part. Someone must have imagined it.

Just before Christmas, Henry bought a fir tree in a pot. Strictly speaking it was a reduced-price reject at the back of the grocery shop and it had grown crooked, drooping towards the left as if it was very tired and straining to lie down. (It made him think of Conor. And once it had made him think of Conor, Henry couldn't just leave it there.) Both Henry and the grocer peered at the tree with their heads tilted to correct the angle. 'I guess you could put a wedge under one side of the pot,' said the grocer. Afterwards Henry hauled it up the communal stairs, shedding needles all the way, getting scratched and nicked, past the boxes and bikes and junk mail and bottles and takeaway packaging and all the other communal things people dumped outside their flats. He drove to a hardware shop on the edge of town and spent an hour trying to find the right Christmas lights and tinsel and baubles.

'These are nice,' the assistant said. She had soft brown eyes and a big ring through her nose as if she were searching for something to be attached to.

'Are they?' he asked.

She laughed. 'Yes. The lights come with a remote control and six different settings. Your sons will like these.' She smiled as she was bagging up his items and asked if he would like to go for a drink, but then she blushed so hard he wondered if he'd misheard. 'See you around,' she said.

Presents were more difficult. There wasn't much money left once the month's maintenance had gone into Debbie's account and he had bought the beds and things for the flat. Henry asked the boys on the phone what they would like, but Conor grunted something that Henry didn't like to ask him to repeat. Owen said he didn't mind what he had for Christmas. He liked everything. When Henry texted Debbie the same question she replied, 'Work it out.'

Henry bought computer games for the boys to play on their laptops. At least it would give them something to do. Passing a sports shop, he noticed a sign advertising cut-price sledges in the shapes of polar bears and penguins. 'They're a bargain, those,' said the manager as he paid. She was a solid-looking, older woman with red hair and a smoker's deep laugh. 'They are made of foam. You can almost lift them with one finger. See?' Henry explained his oldest son was fifteen and too old for sledges, but the woman gave another of her manly laughs. 'No one's too old for snow,' she said. When Henry told his sister on the phone about the animal-shaped sledges, she sighed. 'Why do you think they were cut-price, sweetheart?' she asked. 'It's never going to snow.'

Henry waited for Debbie at the motorway service station. 'They didn't want to come,' she said, squeezing past a Krispy Kreme Doughnut display case. The place was heaving with Christmas travellers. Conor and Owen trailed after Debbie like two shadows, one long and slow, one jumpy and small. Debbie extended her cheek mid-air. 'I'm just warning you.' To Henry's surprise, she accepted his offer to buy refreshments and they crammed, all four of them, around a laminated table, with paper cups the size of vases and drinks that were an angry shade of orange.

'Well,' he said, because no one else was saying anything, they were just staring at their phones and scratching their heads. 'Just like old times.'

'Are you for real?' said Debbie. She wore a dark lipstick, a colour he had never seen her use before, so that her mouth looked as though she'd eaten too many blackberries.

Was he for real? Henry had no idea any more. What was real? In this particular instance, he was being nice, he was saying words for the sake of saying them, and maybe that was not real. Two years ago, when things were at their worst, he had seen motorbikes thundering up and down the hall stairs. He had seen them and heard them, he had smelt the acrid heat of exhaust fumes and petrol, and even though no one else had experienced motorbikes on the hall stairs, it had not made them any less real at the time. It had been terrifying.

'You think I look funny,' Debbie said.

'I don't,' he said.

'Then stop staring at my mouth.'

She had a new fluffy pink Christmas jumper that clung to her. It seemed to have a picture of a knitted squirrel on the front eating some sort of sequinny nut, but he didn't like to peer too closely after what she'd said about her mouth.

'Are you going straight from here to the airport?' he asked.

Debbie didn't reply. She just sucked expansively on her straw and waved her hand as if she were shooing him along.

He said, 'Have you checked your flight? Only there were problems on Christmas Day. A baby was born at the airport.' Conor grunted. Owen gave a smile. Debbie rolled her eyes.

'The computers went down,' she said. 'There was a technical glitch.'

At another table a young woman greeted a man holding a child. He kissed her quickly and passed the child over like a package he'd been finding way too heavy. In the corner, four children wearing Santa hats ate burgers, whilst their parents stood on either side of the table, facing outwards. How many of these people were travelling together and how many were divorced, like himself and Debbie, exchanging children – the only thing left of their marriages – for Christmas?

'I've got a turkey, boys,' he said. 'Tomorrow morning I thought we could do the full works. Presents under the tree. Christmas lunch . . .' The boys glanced up briefly and then returned to their phones.

'They only eat sausages,' interrupted Debbie. 'And pizza.'

'I didn't know they only ate sausages. When did that happen?'

'When you ran off to find yourself. How's that going?'

'Well. You know . . .'

'I haven't a clue,' she said.

Debbie smacked the lid down on her drink and pushed the cup to one side, and Henry couldn't help feeling he was somewhere inside that cup, all set to be cleared away. 'Are you ready?' She slotted a piece of gum in her mouth and stood.

He walked at a short distance behind Debbie and the boys to her new car. Overhead the clouds shifted forward like huge flat plates, tipping one by one over the edge of the horizon. Cars were stuffed with suitcases and bedding and presents. When Debbie passed over the boys' hold-all bags from the boot, she dropped them mid-air as if she couldn't see Henry but expected him to be there none-theless. He couldn't help noticing her suitcase. 'Sun and yoga,' she'd said. Along with, 'Be a father for once.' He wondered if she was going alone or with friends, or maybe someone in particular.

'Boys,' she said. 'I want a quick word with Henry. Go and wait by his car.'

Conor and Owen trundled to one side, reluctant to be out of hearing. Debbie stepped so close to Henry that he could smell the spearmint of her chewing gum. He looked at her hands in order to avoid staring at her sequinny jumper or her blackberry mouth. She seemed to be ripping a serviette into shreds. Her voice said very clearly into his left ear, 'I am warning you. If you do one weird thing while I am away, I will come down on you like a ton of bricks. Do you understand?'

'Yes,' he said. And then he said it again in case the first one didn't sound big enough. 'Yes. I understand.'

'The boys say you keep promising snow.'

'That's only a joke, Debbie.'

She stopped chewing. She clenched her molars very tight. 'Is it?'

'Of course it is.'

'You promise me you're OK? You're not seeing any weird shit?'

Owen must have heard her swear because he crumpled his mouth to suggest he hadn't.

'I promise you I am not seeing anything weird or shitty. That was a long time ago, Debbie. My life these days is numbingly average.'

The boys were silent in the car. Henry could see Conor in the rear-view mirror, scratching his black mop of hair as he hunched over his phone. Owen sat with his anorak zipped all the way to the tip of his chin, and his small hands on his lap, gazing out of the window. It was only once they turned off the motorway that he said solemnly, 'Hm. I don't see any snow yet, Henry.'

Henry's stomach gave a turn; and it still came as a shock that the boys no longer called him Dad, that since his breakdown they'd chosen to call him by his name, as if he were someone they'd met recently and needed to be polite to. 'Well, you know,' he said. 'It might not . . . you know . . . it probably won't . . .'

A sudden movement in the rear-view mirror caused him to stop speaking. It was Conor. The boy swiped his fringe from his eyes. His jaw was as firm and pale as a clenched fist. 'Of course it won't snow,' he shouted and his voice splintered. 'Every time we asked, you *promised*. Do you think we're *kids*?' It was the most comprehensive sentence he'd said in a year and he sounded like a man. A man-version of Debbie.

'Actually, Henry,' said Owen, 'we like turkey as well as sausages.' He tugged a small Tupperware box from his anorak pocket and snapped off the lid. 'Also dried apricots,' he said, beginning to suck on one. He scratched his head amply. 'Did Mum say we have nits?'

'She didn't.'

'We do.'

They fell silent again.

That night seemed to go on and on; from one thirty, when Henry put the turkey in the oven to slow-cook (he'd found a recipe online: twelve hours on a low heat, it said) and crept into his sleeping bag on the sofa, until five, when he at last allowed himself to get up and make coffee, he slept fitfully, stirring awake to open his eyes and look into the darkness, terrified of making a mistake with the boys, asking himself over and over how he would entertain them for five more days. Everything about the flat seemed different now that the boys were inside it. Even the air around him felt taut and fragile. The only thing that remained composed was the snow picture. The young woman waiting in her red coat.

Henry checked the bedroom, easing the door open just an inch or two, but the boys were still fast asleep – the sprawling mass of Conor in the lower bunk, the small sepulchre tidiness of Owen on top. When his sister had rung the night before to ask how things were going, he'd said, 'Fine.' He didn't mention that Conor had been on his phone the whole evening or that Owen had expressed polite surprise that there was no bath in the flat, only a shower, or that when Henry hovered at the bedroom door to call goodnight neither of the boys seemed inclined to call it back. He closed the door gently, as if even that was in danger of fragmenting.

In the sitting room, Henry wriggled on his stomach beneath the tree and switched on the Christmas lights. He arranged the presents to make it look as if there were more of them, resting the two big ones, the sledges, at the back and the smaller computer games in front, and making sure the labels were clearly visible. He began a backward manoeuvre by shifting his weight from one elbow to the other, only somehow he must have knocked the wedge that was holding the tree erect because it gave a sudden sideways lurch as if it had been felled. Henry reached out to rescue it but it was like grabbing hold of a shrub of pins. The only way to steady it was to remain on all fours with it digging into his shoulders, as if he was giving it a piggyback, while he tried to work out what to do next.

'What are you up to, Henry?' From beneath the tree, Henry spied two small feet at the doorway. Pale and perfect as two blue stones.

'Ah. I am fixing the tree, Owen.'

'Mm, it does look wonky.'

'Could you possibly pass me the wedge?'

'I don't see a wedge, Henry. I only see a piece of newspaper folded over and over and over.'

'Yes, that is my wedge.'

'I see.' The feet pattered forward several paces, stopped and then advanced towards the tree. There was a pause during which Henry felt the tree grind its prickled weight from his left shoulder towards his right; it was like being embraced by a giant porcupine. A small hand emerged holding the newspaper, carefully refolded into its wedge shape, only somehow even neater, even more efficient.

'Did it snow in the night?' asked Owen, as Henry stood and brushed down his shoulders.

'I don't think so.'

'Maybe tomorrow?'

'Well, now . . .'

'I'll take a look out of your window.'

Henry watched his son pull back the corner of the curtain. Street lamps were on all over the city like a blanket of orange buttons and the sky glowed a dull neon. Owen didn't believe in Father Christmas – Debbie had wanted the boys to know the truth when they were as young as five; the whole Christmas thing was a rip-off, she said – but it seemed Owen still believed in the magic of an overnight snowfall. The transformation, while he slept, of the world from ordinary to a perfect coating of ice. And so do I, thought Henry. I still want that too. I want the world to be bigger and more mysterious than it is.

Owen turned from the window. 'No snow. Not today.' A solid knot caught in Henry's throat. Owen said, 'I think something is burning in your kitchen, Henry.'

So the online recipe was wrong. The Christmas lunch was cooked and ready – actually it was more than cooked, it was incinerated – and it was not yet seven thirty in the morning. Henry carved off the blackened skin and wrapped what was left of the bird in foil. He could feel his back breaking into a sweat. He needed air.

'Are you all right?' asked Owen. He scanned Henry with a careful look, as if he were afraid bits of his father might fall off. It broke Henry's heart.

He said, 'We should wake Conor and go for a walk. There's a nice park near here. It might be fun.'

'No, thank you. We are too old for parks. But you go. I'll wait.'

'I can't possibly leave you on your own.'

'I'm eleven. Mum leaves us all the time.' Owen lowered himself beside the tree with his knees tucked beneath his chin and his hands touching his feet. He gazed at the presents. 'Four of them seem to be for me,' he said. His mouth hoisted into a beautiful smile like the curve of a new moon.

It was just getting light. The streets were still empty, only bin bags collecting in piles. To the east, a silver light had crept into the sky, and buildings were beginning to take shape through the dark. Henry entered the park gates and made his way towards the bandstand. He walked because it would be less noisy than running, but his head wanted him to run. He had no idea why he'd lied to the boys about snow. Yes, it had started as a joke, but it had become a way of saying all sorts of other more complicated things like *I love you* and *I am sorry I messed up* and *I miss you.* Of all the promises to make, why had he chosen one he couldn't possibly fulfil? He thought of those sledges wrapped under the Christmas tree and groaned out loud.

Henry was visited by one of those memories that prickle the skin. He saw himself as a child, asking his mother whether Father Christmas was real. He watched her pucker her mouth and stare at her shoes and admit briskly that no, he wasn't. 'What about the tooth fairy?' he had asked a while later, still hopeful of a yes in that department. No, not the tooth fairy either. Jack Frost? (Did he seriously believe in Jack Frost? his mother laughed. Yes, he did. He had even seen pictures: a tall man dressed in white with a spike-frozen beard and fingers like claws.) The man in the moon? Was *he* real? 'Get away with you,' she'd said. What about God, then? he'd asked, feeling more and more shaky. Angels? Jesus? His mother reached for a cigarette and snapped her lighter. 'Run along now,' she said. 'This is getting plain silly.' It was like walls toppling down, first one truth and then another, until there was nothing left but grown-up wasteland. The world seemed an entirely more prosaic place and also one without any hope of salvation. Henry felt bereft. He had watched Bea open her Christmas stocking. 'Isn't Father Christmas *wonderful*?' he'd asked, as if she alone held the

155

cup of make-believe now and he might drink a little, if she would only let him. Bea had tossed him a scornful look. 'Don't you *know*?' she'd said. 'Father Christmas is not *real*. I saw his hat in my piano teacher's car.'

Across the park, the large Georgian mansions with gardens that backed on to it stood moored like battle ships, their lights sparkling. They were so vast and beautiful and immovable; their certainty made Henry feel even more insubstantial. He imagined the people inside. All those clever, wealthy people, who never made mistakes, who never had breakdowns, or failed in their marriages, or lost touch with their sons. Henry crossed the grass and then walked around the pond, until he was standing only fifty metres from the gardens. He stopped.

At first he believed it was some kind of nasty joke. He turned to see if anyone was watching, but he was alone, not even a dog-walker in sight. Henry closed his eyes. He counted to twenty, calmly, and breathed deeply, just like it said in those books his sister was always giving him. He opened his eyes and wanted to shout. Where the other gardens showed barren black branches and scribbles of twigs, with barely a leaf in sight, there was one garden, just one, that was completely different. Henry looked up at the sky to check he was not mistaken, but no – the dawn was pale grey, a few rogue stars still shining, the moon no more than a muzzy smudge. Turning back to the garden, Henry felt a low flutter of dread.

It had snowed. Yes, in one garden alone, it had snowed. And not just a little drift, not just a sprinkling. It was a proper snow scene, an almost exact replica of his picture in its clip-on frame at the flat. No matter how many times Henry rubbed his eyes and poked them with his fingers, no matter how many times he shook his head, it didn't go away. He saw snow, snow, nothing but snow.

Slicks of soft white clung to the bare trees. The grass was a thick white duvet. A sagging canopy of clematis had clearly become unmoored by the weight of new snow, and icicles hung like glass fingers from the railings. There was even a criss-cross of slim iced shards above a drain where water had frozen as it spewed from the pipes. Snow sat on the ironwork of a bench and outlined every detail of its pattern in a thick crust. At the far end of the garden, where it met the house, the snow was overhung with shadow and glowed a pale whitish-blue. From a top window a light fell upon the snow garden like a yellow lantern. When he thought he caught a stab of red up there, as if someone had noticed and was looking down, Henry couldn't bear any more. He fled.

Throughout the morning, Henry's mind kept returning to the snow garden. It couldn't have been real. No other garden had snow and there was no snow anywhere else in the park. It made no sense, and yet he had seen it. He didn't dare mention the garden to his sister when she rang to check how he was getting on. He certainly mustn't breathe a word of it to the boys; Debbie would never forgive him. Every time he thought of it, he felt sick with nerves.

'Can we open our presents now?' asked Owen.

Even though the boys had opened their presents in five minutes ('What is this, Henry?' 'It's a polar bear, Owen.' 'Cool,' said Owen. Conor said nothing), and even though Henry's present from his sister was another self-help book (*Learn to Relax and Enjoy Life Again by Embracing Stress and Fear*), the rest of the day went better than Henry expected. He carved the turkey into slices, just like he used to do in the old days, and he served Christmas lunch to the boys with his new plates and cutlery. He drank one small glass of wine and after lunch he played a board game with Owen, while Conor tried out his new computer game. Owen told Henry about the gifts they had received back at home. Nike trainers and a new phone for Conor; Owen had received a jambox and an iTunes voucher.

'I bought the new album by X,' he said.

'What is X?'

Owen laughed. 'Do you really not know?'

'X is only the most famous person ever,' grunted Conor.

'X is a person?' asked Henry. Once he had known everything about his sons, but now there seemed to be so much about their lives he couldn't grasp, as if a child's development required the simultaneous diminishing of the parent.

Owen said, 'X does the Christmas song that goes with your picture. He's number one all over the world.'

At the mention of the snow picture, Henry's pulse began to beat so hard he could hear it. He affected a laugh, only it came out sounding tinny. 'I've never heard of X,' he said.

'By the way, this is for you.' Owen produced from his pocket a small, flat parcel, wrapped in crumpled paper with pictures of reindeers. 'I made it at school.'

Conor flumped impatiently from one side of the sofa to the other.

It was a photograph of the two boys, mounted in a homemade paper frame. Owen had drawn pencil Christmas trees and sledges, laden with splodges of snow. In the photograph the two boys sat side by side, not quite touching, neither of them smiling. They seemed uncertain and very much alone.

'Well, gosh,' said Henry. He would keep it for ever.

*

Henry returned to the park early the following morning. He'd barely slept. In the middle of the night it had seemed frighteningly clear that he had imagined the garden as a result of the snow picture and that he was on the verge of a possible relapse. And yet he also knew that over the past two days he had felt more alive than he'd felt since moving into the flat. He found himself dressing quickly in the dark – and then floundering at the last minute, unable to make the simple choice between a brown wool hat and a blue one. As he fastened his coat, his fingers trembled around the buttons. He eased open the door to the boys' bedroom, but they were asleep.

The sky was too clouded for stars. The buildings were tall, dark shapes in the gloom. Faint sounds came from them as he passed – a telephone ringing, someone playing music. He was glad to see a few lights in kitchens and bedrooms. They made him feel not quite so alone, though he was relieved to be the only person entering the park. As Henry reached the bandstand, he was aware of a jumping and realized it was his blood. He pictured the boys asleep in their bunk beds, he pictured the photograph Owen had given him, and he found himself running. Just one check that the snow garden was not there and he would hurry back to the flat before they woke.

The garden was exactly as he remembered, only more

so. If anything the snow seemed deeper and more perfect. It glowed in the blue dawn light, so soft and pale it could be made of feathers. When a back door opened and a woman stepped out in a red coat, Henry felt his body grow weak. His hands seemed to hang from his arms on string. He walked away, trembling hard. It was everything he could do to stop his teeth from chattering. He took himself for a coffee in order to collect his thoughts, but every time he let his mind drift he saw the snow garden and the woman in her red coat. It was only when the waitress asked if he was waiting for someone, because actually she needed the table, that he realized she'd already delivered his drink and it had gone stone cold.

By the time Henry returned to the flat, the boys were sitting at the table with a packet of sliced bread and a jar of peanut butter between them. They stared up at him as if they'd been waiting for days. 'Where have you been?' asked Conor peevishly, but his eyes were sore as if he had rubbed them too hard and Henry's heart lurched.

'Mum rang,' said Owen.

'What did she say?'

'She said, "How's it going?" Then she said, "Where's Henry?"'

'What did you say?'

'I said, "He is wearing his blue hat."'

'Why did you say that, Owen?'

'I saw you leave. I was trying to keep you out of trouble.'

'Are we in your way or something?' snapped Conor.

Yet despite the awful beginning, the day passed smoothly. Henry made no mention of the snow garden or the woman he had imagined in her red coat. Owen fetched his jambox and played the album by X he had bought with his voucher. He told Henry about the Christmas song that went with his picture – X was one of those very special singers that everybody liked, he said. Even grannies.

'What? Even Conor?' asked Henry, and to his surprise Conor laughed.

'Mum fancies X,' giggled Owen.

In the afternoon, Conor asked if Henry would like to play his computer game, and when Henry suggested that later they could go for pizza and the cinema, the boys agreed they would prefer to stay in and eat leftover turkey. Before they showered, he bought nit treatment. Afterwards he helped them wash it out and combed their hair with a special long-toothed comb. Catching sight later of his two boys, their wet hair flat against their scalps, their backs to him as they watched the television in their pyjamas, Henry paused. Suddenly he experienced the feeling that he had done everything he could and he saw that it was enough.

That night, once he knew Owen was asleep, Henry leant his head against the railing of the top bunk and told his son about the snow garden. He just wanted to describe it, that was all. He needed to get the words and pictures out of his head. In a soft voice, he detailed the trees laden with white and the icicles on the gutters and railings, and as he did, he watched Owen's sleeping face. It had been years since he'd felt the way he had in the past few days – so alive and energized. The boys were his first thought every morning and his last thought every night. Even in his sleep they seemed to come to him in strange dreams where he played board games with them and listened to their music, or told them about his childhood. In fact, had he ever felt this way? Maybe he had forgotten over the years, but it seemed to him this contentment was all new.

He leant over to kiss Owen. It was only as Henry walked away that he realized he had told his son he loved him. The words had just come and they were easy, that was the thing. They were soft as falling snow.

The next day was the boys' fourth with Henry. It was hard to believe they were already over halfway through their visit. Briefly he wondered about the snow garden, but told himself he could not go back again; there was no excuse.

It was not there and the woman in the red coat was an illusion. His boys, on the other hand, were real. He mustn't blow what he had begun to find with Conor and Owen. Once he had returned them safely to Debbie, he would make a doctor's appointment. He would admit he had started to see things again and face the consequences.

And so it came as a shock when the door swung open and the two boys appeared in anoraks, a woollen bobble hat on Owen and a beanie hat in Conor's hand. They had their new sledges. Owen held his proudly. Conor carried his under one arm, like something that he had picked up without really noticing. He couldn't look at Henry and kept jutting his chin as if he were embarrassed but still wanted to be there.

'I thought you could take us to see that garden,' said Owen. 'The one with snow.'

'Oh no,' said Henry, getting up quickly. 'I couldn't. I can't.'

'Why not?'

'Because it's . . . private. You know? It would be trespassing. I can't.' He could feel his skin turning clammy, his pulse racing.

In silence, Owen unzipped his anorak and pulled off his bobble hat. His hair stuck out in a static halo, so blond it was practically white. It was too much. Henry should never have mentioned the garden, just as he should never have promised snow in the first place. He should never have bought the picture—

'Fucking crap!' shouted Conor, throwing down both the beanie and the sledge. 'What's the fucking point of snow if you won't show us?'

'Since when did you swear at home?' asked Henry, taken aback.

'Since when did you become a prick?' said Conor.

Henry strode at such a pace the boys had a struggle to keep up. Their sledges kept getting in their way, but he didn't care. He wanted his sons to suffer a little because it would be nothing compared with the disappointment they had coming. Then he noticed a woman on a street corner staring hard at the boys in their winter woollens and carrying their new sledges, when it was so mild, and Henry felt a flash of indignation. He slowed right down.

'Do you need help, boys?' he said.

'We can manage,' said Conor.

'Thank you,' added Owen.

They turned into the park.

The grass shone blue in the dawn light. The trees were dust against the sky. It was only over to the east, where the sun rose, that the cloud had ripped open to reveal a single streak of henna red.

If only the walk would last longer. Even from the gates, Henry could see the lights of the Georgian mansions sparkling in the distance. As he led the boys past the bandstand and then the pond, Henry felt his limbs begin to weaken and that low feeling of dread in his chest. His breath seemed to be on the verge of stopping altogether. He couldn't look up any more. He could only stare at his feet.

'I see snow!' That was Owen.

'Jeez Louise!' That was Conor.

So there it was, the snow garden. Exactly as Henry had remembered, and exactly as he had seen in his picture. A fairy-tale world, the trees adorned with thick pillows of white, the ground a smooth blanket of bumps and humps. The icicles poked from the railings in transparent points, and drops of frozen moisture clung to the stems like glass beads. And in the middle of it stood a woman in a red coat. He didn't know whether to laugh or cry, the two things seemed so joined up. He felt light-headed. He was afraid he might faint.

Catching sight of Henry, the woman lifted her arm and waved. 'I've seen you here before, haven't I?' she called. Her voice was surprisingly slow and deep. She moved closer to the railing, her shoes making no sound in the snow except the occasional creak. She was older than Henry had expected, her skin very soft and creased, her silvering hair swept into an elegant pleat, but something about the way the snow shone up into her face made her appear both beautiful and bold. Now that he was close to her, he could see that her coat was more of a fleece jacket, with a little logo of an X sewn in silver just below the lapel. She'd pulled the zipper up to her chin.

'Do you actually know her?' whispered Conor.

'Hello there,' piped up Owen.

'These are my sons,' explained Henry. His voice seemed thick in his throat. It was hard to get the words out.

'Would they like to come in?'

Henry faltered. 'I don't think so. I wouldn't want to trouble you . . .'

'Yes,' interrupted Conor.

'Yes, please!' sang Owen. He glanced over his shoulder at Henry and beamed.

The woman took a key from her jacket pocket and slotted it into a section of the railing. A gate opened smoothly.

'Do come in,' she said.

Conor nodded his thanks and shuffled through,

followed by Owen. They clutched their sledges close to their stomachs like floats. Henry stayed on the park side, watching.

'Go ahead,' said the woman in her red coat. 'You enjoy it. No one else has. It was done for a photo shoot and then the record company changed their minds and cancelled. It'll be gone soon. They're coming with giant vacuums to suck it up.'

The boys walked carefully at first, unsure whether the ground beneath them was solid or only ice. Turning, they looked back at the prints their feet had made and laughed. They reached out their hands and tentatively touched the cottony domes of snow on the branches. They knelt to scoop it in their hands and as they grew in confidence they dared to throw it at one another in handfuls that drifted through the air like furry tufts. Owen picked up a small sprig and lifted it to his mouth.

'Don't eat it!' yelled Henry.

The woman in her red fleece laughed. 'It's completely safe. Apparently it's made of the same paper they use for cigarettes. Some batches even taste of menthol. They're nice boys. I'm glad you told them about my garden. It's good to see them playing here.'

Henry nodded. What was this strange bubbling feeling in his belly? 'You may not understand,' he said, 'but this is

168

a major result.' He began to laugh and once he started he couldn't stop.

Henry stood close to the woman in her red coat, watching and laughing as his boys threw down their sledges and fell on them, sliding themselves forwards with their hands. There was no need to say anything else. Briefly he turned and looked back at the park, and even the ordinariness of it was beautiful. Suddenly, out of nowhere, he was so tired. He honestly believed he could stretch right out on the bleached winter grass and sleep for hours.

Henry felt a warm small hand in his, touching his fingertips, and then taking hold of his fingers and squeezing tight. But the voice that came with it was not the high singing voice of Owen, but one that was altogether more cracked and unsure.

'We just want to spend time with you, Dad.'

'Guess what, Mum?' said Owen that night. 'We're going for Chinese food on New Year's Eve. Also, it snowed here.' Owen stopped suddenly and handed his phone to Henry. 'She wants a word,' he said quietly. He bit his lip. Conor shuffled forwards, pulling a face at Owen. Henry pressed Owen's phone to his ear.

'Hello, Debbie,' he said.

'It snowed?' It was less a question, more an accusation.

'In a manner of speaking, yes.'

There was a pause, during which he imagined her taking a deep breath. Grinding her teeth. Instead she laughed. 'You jammy bastard. How come you fixed that?'

Somewhere there must be an explanation – there was always an explanation, just as there was always a word for something if you searched hard enough. You could call it luck, intuition, the gods, magic, or you could be very practical if you wished and call it mashed-up paper – but this time Henry had no inclination to give it a name and understand. There was something sublime about what had happened, something small and beyond words.

It had snowed at Christmas, just as Henry promised. That was enough.

I'll Be Home for Christmas

'Now remember, everybody!' calls Sylvia, raising her voice and hitting a thin note, 'X doesn't want any fuss! Just a normal family Christmas! Can you all hear me?'

She looks out over the sea of paper party hats and her heart swoops. Sylvia doesn't even recognize half the people in her sitting room. Last time she checked, there were cars parked the length of the street. All three bedrooms have been commandeered for the guests' coats. She has no idea where X will put his suitcases when he arrives.

The pale, stick-thin girls in red fleeces with a large silver embroidered X on the back are from the record company. They gape at their phones because apparently they're all tweeting. Earlier Sylvia offered them coffee, and to her dismay they said yes, please, to caffeine-free drinks only, so she had to send her daughter Mary rushing out for herbal tea bags and now Mary is in such a fury she is the only person in the room who refuses to wear her party hat.

As for the others, it's anyone's guess why most of them are here. Some haven't seen X since he was a little boy; others have never even met him. A few are something to do with Sylvia's sisters. (Diane, Sylvia's eldest sister, is dressed in a new blue trouser-suit, matched with a silk blouse that shows off her figure perfectly. Linda, the middle sister, has come straight from her hairdresser; she has chosen a chic style with one side of her hair cut two inches lower than the other. Whenever she speaks to her, Sylvia has to stop herself from tilting to the left.) Every chair in the room is occupied by at least two distant relatives. There are ageing great-aunts and uncles squashed against the walls; there are cousins and second cousins packed into the bay window, and brothers-in-law, nieces, nephews and their extended families jammed around the dining table. Sylvia's mother is wedged on the sofa, sandwiched between two staff members from the nursing home, and several children are already tucking into the buffet. Meanwhile a dog – who on earth brought a dog? – is chewing something in the corner.

Sylvia claps her hands. She chirrups again, 'X just wants us all to be *normal*! All right, everyone?' She can barely breathe for excitement.

Across the room, Malcolm averts his eyes and gives a

long sigh that seems to be aimed at his Hush Puppies. Mary crushes a brand-new cushion to her stomach. She is dressed from head to toe in black. She hasn't even brushed her hair.

'I'm tired, Mum,' X had said a few days ago on the phone. 'I miss you guys. I think I'll come home for Christmas.'

But they'd already *had* Christmas, she'd laughed. She didn't mention that she'd waited all day for a call.

'Oh,' he said, as if he should have spotted that. 'Yeah.' The signal had gone before she could say anything else. When she re-dialled, his phone went straight to voicemail. She tried again and again and every time it was the same. If only she hadn't pointed out that he'd missed Christmas. How could she have been so ordinary?

'Something's wrong,' she'd said, waking in the middle of the night and snapping on the bedside lamp.

'Do you have indigestion, Sylv?' Malcolm reached for his reading glasses. (How were *they* going to help?)

'We need to ring X.'

'Sex?' he'd said, blinking. He looked all puffy with sleep and vaguely alarmed.

'X,' she said. 'Your son?'

'You mean Tim?'

'I mean X.'

'But he's fine. He's good. He's Christmas number one all over the world. Please can we go back to sleep?'

'Sleep?' she'd exclaimed. '*Sleep?* You'd sleep if the house was burning down. We have to ring him right now. We have to invite him home for Christmas.'

'We've *had* Christmas, Sylvia.' The remark sounded even worse now that she heard Malcolm saying it. 'Don't you think one Christmas is enough?'

'We're going to have another one. These days families do it all the time. Here,' she said, passing him the bedside phone. 'It's ringing.'

'I thought *you* were speaking to him.'

'He might think I'm fussing.'

'You *are* fussing.'

'Just speak, will you?'

She'd heard X's gentle voice at the end of the phone, 'Hey, Dad?' and her heart fluttered. She'd never understood the phrase until X became famous, but whenever she heard him or even thought about him, her heart really did seem to have a life of its own. 'Where are you, son?' Malcolm had asked. Sylvia had flattened her ear against Malcolm's bristly, warm neck and heard X say, 'I dunno, Dad. It could be China. I've forgotten.' How could your child be so far from where he'd started? It was as if a little piece of Sylvia was spinning out there, a brilliant shiny piece that she barely recognized, in somewhere that might (or might not) be China.

'Tell him to come home for Christmas,' she whispered violently.

Of course, if she had made the phone call herself, she would have asked practical questions – What would you like to eat? How many days will you be staying? – but Malcolm asked none of those things. Instead he established that X would be home in two days and he wanted nothing special, just a normal family Christmas. 'Ask if he'd like turkey,' she hissed, flapping her hands. 'And trimmings.'

'Bye then, son,' yawned Malcolm.

'What did he say? What does he want?'

Malcolm smiled so fondly it turned into a one-eyed wink. 'You heard every word, Sylv. He said, "Nothing special." He doesn't want a fuss, love.'

'But he hasn't been home for six months. What about a finger buffet?'

'A finger buffet is a fuss.'

'Yes, I'm sure he'd love a finger buffet,' she said.

Nothing special, she reminded herself as she scanned her cookery books for recipes early the next morning, and none of them seemed quite good enough for the most famous son in the world. 'Nothing special,' she said

177

casually to her sisters, phoning at midday and mentioning the buffet as if she'd only just remembered. '*Nothing special*,' she whispered as she whipped up dips and mince pies, cheesy straws, sausage rolls, gingerbread biscuits cut into snowflakes and iced, all those things he'd loved as a child; as she stuffed another turkey for the cold meats platter and steamed a Christmas pudding.

'You haven't invited anyone else for the buffet, have you?' asked Malcolm, discovering the glazed ham in the fridge as well as a Tupperware tub of Coronation Chicken, sixty vol-aux-vents and a poached salmon.

'Only my sisters,' said Sylvia. She didn't mention that her sisters had suggested inviting all those other extended members of the family. She was given to saying things that weren't entirely true but would be simpler if they were.

'I don't see what the fuss is about,' said Mary.

Sylvia bought new cushions for the sitting room – well, they were looking tired, the old ones, it was time for a change – and a set of special Christmas mats for the dining table and matching red napkins, along with bumper boxes of paper hats and those little party poppers. '*Nothing special*,' she hummed, vacuuming the house from top to bottom, polishing windows, scouring the sink and the bath and the two toilets. '*Nothing special*,' she said out loud, arriving home from the garden centre with so many potted poinsettias in her arms she failed to spot Malcolm's slippers in the hall and practically split her head open as she crashed into the door frame. 'Nothing special,' she reminded her sisters when they rang to discuss what they should make for the buffet table, sweet or savoury?

'But I can manage,' Sylvia told them.

'We'll bring both,' her sisters said.

'You never do this when I come home,' said Mary, glancing up from the sofa as Sylvia added a few extra baubles to the tree. Mary was using one of the new cushions as a footrest.

'But you're only coming from Aberystwyth. We see you every weekend, Mary.'

'Oh? So you'd buy party hats if I stayed away like Tim and never rang—'

'He's called X,' said Sylvia. 'He doesn't want to be called Tim.'

'You're as bad as everyone else,' said Mary to her magazine. There was a picture of X on the front cover. He was laughing, his image superimposed on the picture that was everywhere, the one of the young woman with her red coat. Sylvia hadn't seen it before. 'And by the way, you know he can't sing?'

'Can I look at that picture, love?' asked Sylvia.

Mary held the magazine in front of her head as if to

make a point. She could be devastatingly unhelpful when she put her mind to it.

Something was different about X's face. It was smoother, more tanned, pointier. Even more refined. Sylvia couldn't help wondering if her sisters had seen the magazine. She'd make sure it was lying somewhere in a casual way – in the kitchen where they would be bound to see it, as if it just happened to be on its way to the recycling and hadn't quite made it. Strange and wonderful to think that only a year ago her son was plain Tim who'd left school without impressing anyone – unlike two of his cousins who were already at Oxford. He couldn't even get a job. He'd spent his time fiddling with his guitar in his bedroom. It was Mary who was the gifted one in the family, the real musician. (Mary and Malcolm, if you counted drums as music, which Sylvia didn't; she made him keep his drum kit in the shed.) It was Mary who was always winning singing competitions at school. The sitting room had been stuffed with her cups and rosettes. Then Tim had posted a few songs on YouTube that scored a million hits, and the next thing they knew a booker was ringing from a late-night music programme – someone had dropped out at the last minute – and Tim ended up stealing the show. 'I'm changing my name,' he'd admitted once he got the record deal. 'X?' she'd repeated. 'X?' 'If I'm Tim,' he'd said, 'I'm *me.*' 'I see,' she'd said, not seeing at all. She hadn't always liked being Sylvia, she'd wanted to be her sisters, but it had never occurred to her that she might swap her name and become altogether shinier. She'd assumed change would be more complicated than that.

And now Sylvia feels her breath gallop as she looks again at the mass of paper hats, like a roomful of bright sails, the eager crowd squashed inside her sitting room. Things *have* changed. These days people stop her in the street, people she doesn't even know, to tell her how much they like her son. And normally the family gathers for Christmas drinks at her sisters' houses because they have the extra space. It's years since they have come to Sylvia's. 'X will be here any moment!' she announces. Carefully she steps between several kneeling nieces and the pale girls from the record company and picks up a bowl of Twiglets. She almost drops it, she's so nervous. She signals to Malcolm with her free hand that it is time to hand out the drinks, but he misunderstands and sends a wave before resuming a conversation with one of the distant cousins. 'Fetch the drinks,' she hisses to Mary.

'Why me?' Mary hisses back.

Whilst Mary fetches the drinks, Sylvia tells stories about X to her mother's nursing staff. They can't get enough. She tells them about the time they took X to see

Thomas the Tank Engine when he was three and how he waved, and the time he fell and cut his knee open and yet he didn't cry once, he just smiled. 'X was always special,' she says. 'You know he met Obama?'

'No!' gasp the nursing staff. They had no idea he'd met Obama.

'Yes,' says Sylvia. 'Obama flew him over to the White House for a private concert. They're huge fans. *Huge.*' And then she says it again, because she is so enjoying the word. 'Really huge.'

'Sylvia, dear, who is X?' pipes up her mother.

'X is Tim, Mother. Remember?'

'Why is Timothy called X?'

'Because he is a very famous pop star.' Sylvia is aware she is talking loudly and everyone is listening. She is aware her voice doesn't sound quite like her own, but a new and brighter, more brilliant voice. 'He is recognized all over the world. He can't even go to the shops.'

'He *never* went to the shops,' says Mary, reappearing with the hostess trolley and the drinks. 'He never left his bedroom.'

'So why isn't he called Timothy?' asks Sylvia's mother.

'We have been through this, Mother. We've been through it a few times. Tim was Timothy, but now Tim is X.' Suddenly she sounds less shiny and more like her old maths teacher. 'So we don't call him Tim any more. We call him X. You see?'

'As opposed to Y,' snarls Mary, passing bottles of beer to the aged uncles. 'Do any of you lot want straws?'

'Tim is called Y?' asks her mother.

'You'd better take a napkin with your Twiglets,' says Sylvia.

The doorbell rings. *Ding dong!* Everyone freezes.

'Oh my God,' shrieks someone young and female. 'It's X!' The dog wags its tail and cocks an ear in the direction of the front door.

'Does everyone have a party popper?' calls Sylvia in a rush, 'Mary, have you got the welcome banner?' Mary gives a twisted grimace as if someone has stamped on her foot, and Sylvia wishes she had given the welcome banner to someone less complicated, like her mother.

Oh, but her mother's paper hat has slipped down over her head and now she is wearing it like a neck brace. She also seems to be falling through the gap between the two nursing staff.

Sylvia is aware, as she moves to the door of the sitting room, as she opens it and sees the outline of her son at the front door, as she turns back to the sea of expectant faces, as she reminds herself to be calm, keep calm, that she has never felt so significant as she does at this moment. All her

183

life she has been overshadowed by her sisters. They were the ones who were clever at school, who had naturally good figures – Sylvia was always inclined to store weight on her hips and tummy – they were the ones who dated clever boys from the grammar school and each married a lawyer. She turns to the crowd and puts her finger to her mouth for quiet and to her amazement they fall silent like a choir waiting for the first drop of the baton. She makes her way down the hall to welcome the most famous son in the world. Her heart beats so hard it is like a thing in her hands.

X stands at the door in a pair of torn jeans and a soft grey T-shirt. He leans against the doorframe, as if he is about to fall asleep. There is something different about him, yes, but it is not the thing she expected and it is so familiar she can't even put her finger on it. 'Hiya, Mum,' he mumbles. He gives a shy smile and so does Sylvia. When she had imagined this scene, she was going to embrace X and somehow everyone would cheer. As it is, she doesn't quite know what to say or even what to do. She slips off her party hat.

A thickset woman wearing another of the record company red fleeces shoves out her hand and grabs hold of Sylvia's. Behind her stands a row of suited men so huge and wide they block out the light. They have no necks to speak of, and they stand in a respectful way with their feet wide and their hands crossed over their genitalia. On *Sleep* mode.

'Hiya, Mrs X,' says the woman in her red fleece. 'I'm Potts. How's things?'

'Good,' says Sylvia. She realizes she is still holding the bowl of Twiglets.

Potts says, 'It's great you could have him. X really needs the rest. He's been . . . you know.'

What? thinks Sylvia. He's been what? Singing a lot? Travelling a lot? She hasn't a clue. And where is his suitcase? He has no baggage whatsoever. He doesn't even have a coat.

'Kinda crazee,' says Potts, supplying the answer. She pulls a face as if she is balancing something tricky just between her eyebrows. Before she can explain any further the sitting-room door swings open and a young woman – Sylvia hasn't a clue who she might be – claps her eyes on X, gasps, and bursts into tears.

'Is she OK?' asks Potts.

The sitting-room door opens a little further. A pair of dismembered hands reaches for the sobbing girl and guides her out of sight. The door snaps shut.

'Do please come inside,' says Sylvia in her best voice.

Potts replies that she has a few things to sort out but

she'll be right back, then slides her mobile phone out of her back pocket and consults it – two hours to take X to the airport.

'Why? Is he doing something at the airport?' asks Sylvia.

Potts laughs as if this is terribly funny. 'He has a flight to catch at nine p.m. The TV crew will be here in an hour.'

'The TV crew?' Side by side with the devastating news about him leaving soon sits this other detail about the television crew. Sylvia has no idea what to say.

'They don't want to do anything *special*. They just wanna film you, like – being normal. It'll be cute.' Potts puckers her mouth as if that last word is spelt *quewt*. 'You don't have to dress up or anything.'

I *am* dressed up, thinks Sylvia.

She says, 'Would any of you . . . ?' (What do you call a bodyguard? How do you address a set of them? Her sisters' children have never had bodyguards.) 'Would any of you *fellows* like to come in?'

'Nah thanks, Mrs X,' says one. 'We'll just keep an eye on things out here.'

As Sylvia turns to her son, she realizes what is different about him. It shocks her, because the thing that is different is that he is *not*. Different. He is not different in any way whatsoever. If anything his skin looks slightly grey and oily, a few spots on his chin. His mouth is small and chapped. His face is nothing like the one on the magazine cover. You could walk past X and not notice him.

Potts strides towards her car – it looks more like a tank with black windows – parked in the middle of the street so that nothing can pass. It is only when she is halfway down the path that she turns, apparently remembering a joke. 'Oh, Merry Christmas, yeah?'

Something happens in the doorway between the hallway and the sitting room. X becomes the boy Sylvia has seen on the television. As she reaches for the door, as she explains that a few of the family have popped by, is that all right, and he says nothing, he only shuffles, she wonders how on earth this is all going to work. But the door swings back, the crowd cheers and suddenly X overtakes her with a fast skip, waving his arms above his head and calling, 'Hiya.' The assembled relatives gasp and touch his sleeve and ask, 'How are you, X, how are you doing?' and he gives an infectious laugh and says that he is *cwool*. 'No shit,' says Diane. (*No shit?* thinks Sylvia. Since when?) *Pop, pop, pop*, crack the party poppers, spewing multicoloured streamers. Whilst everyone else in the room is a dull monochrome, X exudes energy, as if he has been plugged into a generator. Even his hair zings. His fingernails. You can feel the heat coming off him.

And maybe a little of his shine falls over Sylvia too, because as she moves behind him, people step back and lower their heads.

I am the mother, she thinks, *of the most famous boy in the world.*

My sisters are not.

She takes them a bowl of oriental snacks. 'The bodyguards are going to stay outside,' she says.

Her sisters look eaten alive with curiosity. Linda's eyebrows leap so far upwards they disappear in her slanting fringe. '*Bodyguards?*'

'Yes. They need to watch out for the camera crew.'

'*Camera crew?*' In her excitement, Diane's new jacket pops open.

Meanwhile, X signs the arm of the girl who sobbed earlier, and then another, and another, and another. He kisses his aunties Diane and Linda and compliments them on their clothes and hair. ('Oh, this old thing!' remonstrates Diane; 'Oh, my awful mop!' giggles Linda. They are reduced to girls. *What about my hair?* thinks Sylvia.) X poses for selfies with all the teenagers, one after another. He pulls faces, just like they do, only instead of appearing foolish, gawky, he looks even more delightful.

Reaching Sylvia's mother, he simply holds her hand.

'Who is ready for the buffet?' calls Sylvia, but this time no one turns.

Malcolm watches his son's progress around the room with his arms crossed and a look of bewilderment, as if the sun is in his eyes.

It is true that something happens to X when he is put in front of a crowd, but it is also true that something happens to the crowd when it is put in front of X. It is a sort of electric combination that amounts to something bigger than its individual parts. But what Sylvia cannot work out is how it has happened. She saw him in the hallway. He was so plain he looked like blotting paper. And now he seems to mean something different to everybody. He is a cool kid to the teenagers; he is a lover to the girls; he is a nice boy to the older relatives; he is a bit of a lad with his aunties. He carries so much baggage, and none of it is his own. And suddenly she can only picture her son buried beneath so many suitcases he is lost to her, which is an irony considering that he appears to travel these days without one of his own.

'Aww, hiya,' croons X, spotting the dog and bending down. Even the dog wags its tail and behaves like a proper TV dog. A wave of mobile phones lifts above paper-hat level and click.

Mary marches up to him. She holds out her arms stiffly. It is hard to tell if she is welcoming him or pushing him away. 'Remember me?' she asks in her tight, difficult way.

X looks up at her from the floor. 'Hiya, sis.'

'*Sis*?' she barks. 'Who *are* you now?'

X looks around the crowd. 'X,' he laughs. And everyone else laughs too. He is X. Of course he is X. What is Mary talking about? The room crackles with a new tension.

'Do you want a beer?' she asks.

'That'd be nice. Cwool.'

'So go find the fridge,' says Mary.

X pales and gives a frightened glance around the room as if he has no idea any more how to do something so simple as finding a fridge. If he seemed before to be plugged in to an invisible source of energy, he seems now to have been disconnected.

'Tim?' calls Mary.

His face is grey, then ashen. He reels, losing his balance. Even his head looks too heavy. His eyelids flicker, open and shut, open and shut. His body gives a jolt.

'Tim?' she repeats.

He crumples, like something folding up on itself, and falls in a heap to the floor.

*

Sylvia fills a pan with water and sets it on the stove. Her son sleeps at the kitchen table with his head cradled in his arms.

It is Mary who has saved the day. It was Mary who cleared a space around X and called to her parents to help him to the kitchen. It was Mary who made a joke about pop stars not being like they used to be in the old days and had all the ageing relatives laughing into their napkins. It was Mary who shouted, 'Who likes charades?' and caused such an uproar when she acted out *Carry on Camping* that several of the elderly uncles had to be escorted to the bathroom. It was Mary, too, who handed round plates and Christmas napkins and galvanized her aunts into helping her dish out the buffet lunch. It was even Mary who called on her father to fetch his drum kit and found her old guitar in X's bedroom and led a singalong of Christmas hits. The last time Sylvia popped her head around the door, even the dog was wearing a paper hat and howling in unison.

An hour and a half has passed and Sylvia has just sat with her boy in the kitchen whilst he sleeps. When the door eases open, she springs forward to block the way, but it's only Malcolm.

'How is he?' he whispers.

She thinks of the way her husband gathered his son

in his arms and lifted him over his shoulder, bearing him out of the sitting room like the tenderest scrap of a child.

Sylvia says, 'OK.' Then she asks how things are in the sitting room and he laughs.

'Mary's having a ball. Everyone is. Nobody seems to mind that he isn't there.' He collects a few more bottles from the fridge and as he reaches the door he says, 'I think there's a TV crew. They're talking to your mother.'

Sylvia blows Malcolm a kiss and he slaps his cheek as if he has just caught it, and then he slips her kiss into his trouser pocket for safe-keeping.

As the water comes to the boil, Sylvia lowers an egg into the pan and sets the timer. She turns to her son, with his head on the table, his mouth a grey O.

'Wakey, wakey,' she whispers. 'I've boiled you an egg for your Christmas dinner.'

He says sleepily, 'I was meant to do a photo shoot. In a garden of fake snow. I flipped. I said I wouldn't do it. It was just some photos in a garden of paper. Why couldn't I do that?'

'You're tired. You're very tired.'

'What am I doing, Mum?' He doesn't move his head. He just rolls his eyes to show that the thing he doesn't understand is all around him. From the sitting room comes the sweet voice of Mary singing that she wishes it could be Christmas every day. Sylvia smiles.

She thinks, *Thank God it isn't. Thank God for the ordinary days.*

Sylvia fetches the bread and carves off the heel. She butters two slices. 'When I was a girl I was always following my sisters. Everywhere I went, it seemed they'd already been there. I had to find something they couldn't do. But what? They could do everything.'

'So what did you do, Mum?'

She pulls the egg out of the boiling water. She places it in the eggcup and cracks it open with a knife. 'I became a singer.'

'*You?*'

She laughs. 'Yes. Me.' She cuts the bread into soldiers and arranges them in a fan-shape on the plate.

'I never heard you sing.'

'No,' she says. 'I was rubbish at that as well.'

They laugh.

Then, 'I don't mind what you do,' she says. 'I'm still proud.'

Sylvia thinks of the roomful of relatives in their party hats. She thinks of the bodyguards outside and Potts in her armoured vehicle and the young girls in their red fleeces. She thinks of all those suitcases she imagined earlier, piled on top of her son, and in her mind she lifts them up, one by one, and returns them to their rightful owners. And there is one that belongs to no one but herself – a suitcase containing all that desire to be bigger and better than her sisters. In her mind, she picks it up. She unpacks it and puts it away.

Sylvia pictures her sisters – Diane in her new suit, Linda with her lopsided hair – and she feels a surge of such love, such tenderness that her throat tightens. She places the egg in front of her son and passes him salt and a teaspoon.

Sylvia's heart beats very slowly, very calmly, like a regular plain old heart, as her son eats his boiled egg, like any regular, plain old son.

Trees

On New Year's Eve, Oliver's father phoned and asked an unlikely question. 'Do you know what I regret about my life?'

Oliver said, 'I've no idea, Dad. Never doing anything?' He was trying to make light of the question because the last thing he needed was a full-blown conversation. Oliver's girlfriend was feeling sick again. He'd opened the windows in the flat but the air felt thick. There just didn't seem to be enough of it. Maybe it was because he and Sal were living all the way up on the fifteenth floor.

Oliver's father gave a soft laugh and changed the subject. So how was the weather?

'Well . . .' said Oliver, staring at the window. The sky was low and heavy and the grey of soft ash. 'It's the same as yesterday. And the day before that.'

'Ah, yes,' said his father, turning serious again.

'How is it with you?'

'Yes, it's the same with me.'

'Right,' said Oliver.

'Yes,' said his dad.

Oliver had always felt let down by his father. He still had a clear memory of asking him to make sandcastles as a little boy and his father failing to move from his deck chair. That was his father, all over. He never moved if he could help it. They had spent a fortnight every summer at the same holiday camp and it wasn't even in the next county, it was half an hour's drive away. As Oliver got older, he had clashed with his father over everything. Television, politics, music, clothes, language – you name it. When Oliver told his father he'd been offered a place at drama school, his father had carried on reading the paper. Didn't he know all actors were gay? his father said later. And Oliver, whose eighteen-year-old mind was constantly on women, who couldn't get enough of them, said, 'Great. I'll get out my leathers.' His mother acted as a bridge between Oliver and his father, and after her death, Oliver rarely went home. He rang every Sunday and they stuck to traffic news or the weather. With those two subjects they seemed safe. Oliver's previous girlfriend had said he should visit his father more often. 'I like him,' she'd said. 'He's just a lonely old man.' But it was all right for her. She'd only met him a few times.

'Actually I was wondering if you might come over,' said his father.

'Now, Dad? It's New Year's Eve.'

'Yes, I know.' His father said nothing after that. It was as if he were simply waiting for Oliver to change his mind. From the silence, it seemed he was prepared to wait a long time.

Oliver began to feel cold. He'd avoided visiting his father over Christmas by pretending that he was filming. The truth was, he was out of work; there'd been nothing since he'd been employed to leap about as a giant bran flake for a breakfast-cereal commercial. He had no idea how he was going to look after Sal and their baby. Christmas dinner had been beans on toast in front of the TV; afterwards, Sal had gone clubbing. A girl needed a break from being pregnant, she'd said. Along with, 'I don't know why I let you talk me into keeping this thing.'

So what was it that his father regretted so much that he needed to see Oliver on New Year's Eve? Was he wishing he had read a book, perhaps, or gone to see a film, or travelled abroad, or done anything that might have challenged him to think a little more deeply? No, apparently his father regretted none of those things. Instead he said, 'I wish I'd planted more trees.'

Oliver dug his fingers through his hair. It was what he did when he was confused. 'Trees?'

'Yes, trees.'

'You didn't plant *any* trees, Dad.'

His father groaned as if he'd been punched. He gave a series of tiny clicks.

'Dad?' said Oliver, beginning to worry.

His father blew his nose. When he spoke, his voice was a broken thing, a querulous whisper. '*Nobody* has planted enough trees. I need twenty of them, Oliver. I need to put things straight.'

Oliver's father had never mentioned the need to plant a tree. He hadn't even mentioned growing a flower. He still lived in the house where Oliver had grown up and the back garden was a mix of crazy paving and buddleia, both of which appeared to look after themselves. Once Oliver's mother had asked for pots to be put in front of the house, because they were nice, they showed a person had style, and his father had filled the narrow strip in front of the window with cement. 'I thought you wanted it clean,' his father said, when his mother saw what he had done and shrieked like a fox. 'I wanted it pretty,' she said. And his father had scratched his head as if he couldn't understand how 'clean' and 'pretty' weren't the same. He was not the gardening type. If a plant had a blossom he called it a flower and if it just had some leaves he called it a weed.

By the time Oliver arrived at his father's house, it was early evening and already dark. His father stood waiting at the bay window. He wasn't even hidden to one side like Oliver's mother used to be, as if she just happened to be there in the front room inspecting the curtains for small signs of wear and tear and Oliver's arrival was the last thing on her mind. His father had lifted the nets and parked himself in full view like a human Christmas tree, only a brown-pullovery one and without any lights.

As Oliver opened the gate (hanging on one hinge) on to the small patch of cement (cracked now) and the latch gave the metallic clunk it had always made, he remembered being a child in that house, waiting for something to happen, for life to get bigger; now it was as if everything had tumbled the other way round and he was the father and his father was the boy. He stooped to pass beneath the doorframe, not because he'd ever bumped his head but because he suddenly felt as if he might.

'Have you got the trees?' his father called from the front room.

The hall smelt of chicken soup. It always did. The smell was a sort of thick, cloudy presence you began to forget once you'd spent time with it but which always came as a shock after you'd been away. When Oliver's mother was alive the house had also smelt of her, a sweet, busy scent, and now that she was gone the chicken-soup smell all on its own was a forlorn thing, as if it too had been widowed.

Oliver said he had. Got the trees.

'Are they good ones?'

'They're trees, Dad. They all look the same. They're in the van.'

His father's socks were drying on the radiator. On the shelf above were several bills and three unopened envelopes from the hospital. TWO DEEP PAN PIZZAS FOR THE PRICE OF ONE (*offer does not include stuffed crust*). A Christmas card had been propped open with the picture of a girl in snow that had been everywhere since November. Oliver was about to steal a look at the message inside when his father appeared.

'I was hoping for apple trees,' his father said. 'Or silver birch.' He wore a checked shirt and pullover but he must have done up the buttons wrong because the left side of the collar had got swallowed in his pullover and the lower right corner of the shirt hung down like a flag. His neck was as scrawny as a little bird's. Had he lost weight? His face certainly had a more solemn look and he had very carefully combed his hair like threads across his scalp. But since when had he become so knowledgeable about trees?

Oliver had already had quite a time of it, with the trees. He'd told Sal about the problem. He'd explained that his father had never mentioned trees before or a need to plant them and that there was something in his voice that had struck Oliver as alarming. She had said, 'What the fuck? It's New Year's Eve. I'm pregnant.' 'I know,' he'd said. 'I know. But he's an old man and you're not due until June.' It was possibly not a kind thing to say and it had not gone down well. Sal had grabbed her parka and stormed out. 'Don't even bother following me,' she'd hissed. After that Oliver had rung a local garden centre because recently he seemed to have got so many things wrong, he felt the need to do just one thing right. He'd asked the man on the phone all about trees and the man had said he could rustle up twenty if Oliver really wanted them. He seemed eager to talk about trees and promised to stay open for another half-hour, even though it was New Year's Eve, until Oliver arrived with the van. Great, said Oliver. Perfect. He hung up.

And then he remembered he no longer had a van.

'You want to borrow it?' said Binny. His ex-girlfriend couldn't seem to look at him. She was very busy concentrating on a spot to the left of his shoulder.

'I'm really sorry, Bin,' Oliver kept saying. And he meant

it, now that she was standing in front of the house where he had spent the happiest three years of his life, now that he saw her again dressed in her green velvet top and loose trousers with a giant pair of blue-monster-feet slippers, he knew how truly sorry he was. For everything.

'Bring it back tomorrow,' she said, passing over the keys.

'I can bring it back in a few hours if you like.'

'I'm not going anywhere. Tomorrow's fine.' They paused, uncertain what to say next. There was a smell in the house he hadn't noticed before, so full it was like another person.

'Rose oil,' said Binny, as if reading his thoughts. 'An old friend of mine came over for coffee. I was worried there'd be nothing between us any more, but I was wrong. There was lots. We laughed and laughed.'

'What's that noise?'

'Oh.' She glanced over her shoulder towards the back door. 'That'll be Coco's goat.'

'She got a goat for Christmas?'

'Don't even ask.' Binny ran her hand through her thick hair. A wedge shot out above her ear and stuck out like a flap, the way it always did. He knew every small thing about her, just as she did about him. He loved her more than anyone.

'Could I see Coco?' he said. 'And Luke? Say hello?'

'I think it's better if you don't.' Briefly Binny caught his eye and gave a smile that seemed to hurt, and then she concentrated again on that interesting spot to the left of his shoulder. 'How's Sally?'

Oliver had no idea how to say, 'Binny, I have made a terrible mistake. Binny, she says she doesn't want to be a mother. Binny, I don't know what to do.' He had no idea how to say, 'Those nights when it was just you and me and the kids and we stayed in playing Scrabble and I cheated and Coco hit the roof, I want them back, Binny. I got it all wrong. I miss you.' So instead he said, 'Fine.' And after that he smiled and shrugged and there was nothing for it except to turn and walk away. He tried to ring Sal to check she was all right but she didn't answer, as he knew she wouldn't, and well, to be honest, it was a relief.

By the time Oliver found the garden centre, it was past five. The owner was furious. He'd been waiting almost two hours. He showed Oliver some twigs in pots, twenty in all. Actually it looked as if he'd shoved a load of dead branches in plastic pots. There wasn't one scrappy leaf between them. And when Oliver had said as much, the guy shouted, 'What the hell? It's winter. Of course they've got no leaves. I waited for you. I gave you the Rolls-Royce treatment and now you're complaining?' He was wearing a flat cap, like an artist, and one earring. And Oliver said, 'I didn't ask for Rolls-Royce treatment, I just asked for trees.' He added that he didn't even like Rolls Royces – or any cars, for that matter. 'The van is my girlfriend's,' he said. And then he began to shake because it dawned on him, as if for the first time, that Binny was not his girlfriend. Sal was. An impy girl who blew up at him for worrying about his father and because he liked porridge at half past nine, who would be the mother of his child in six months. He thought of Binny, leaning against her doorframe, her shoulders soft inside her velvet top, her smile that was simultaneously generous and girlish so that it scrunched up her whole face. To his shame, his eyes began to blur.

And the tree guy had said, 'Look, I'm sorry, mate. It's been a bad time. What with Christmas and everything. People only want decorations. I run a garden centre and all I sell are nasty home furnishings. It gets to me. And we've had no rain for days. It makes my job harder, you see.'

And Oliver said, 'No, I'm sorry. It's my fault. It's been tricky for me, too.' He didn't even like trees, he added. The remark was meant to show the man he was over the tears. It was meant to make the man laugh.

It didn't.

The tree man had given him such a sad look, as if he'd

seen right into Oliver's chest, where his heart should be, and found a ragged wound, and he'd said quietly, 'Well, that's a shame, you know.' He had touched Oliver's hand very gently, like a friend who wanted to help. 'You know, I think you may have made a terrible mistake,' he said. Oliver had no idea whether he was referring to the trees or Binny or the baby or something altogether more spiritual.

So he hadn't asked what kind of trees they were.

Or what kind of twigs, for that matter.

He had just fished in his pocket and paid for the things.

However, his father was surprisingly excited. He didn't question their size, or the issue of no leaves. He left Oliver in the hallway and made his way through to the kitchen, holding on to the walls as he passed as if he were just checking they were still where they should be.

Did Oliver have any John Innes No. 2? he called.

Who's he? Oliver asked.

His father laughed from the kitchen. 'The special soil.' You needed John Innes No. 2 to plant a tree, apparently. And what about supports for the trees?

No, Oliver said. He didn't have any of those things.

The lino had begun to curl on the hall floor. You could see the bare wood beneath. And there were dark patches in the woodchip wallpaper that hung like shadows on an X-ray.

'How was Christmas?' called his father. 'How is that nice woman?'

'What nice woman?'

'The one you live with. With those nice kids.'

'Oh,' said Oliver.

The house was beginning to deteriorate, like his father's lopsided shirt and the chicken-soup smell and the strip of concrete outside, and like Oliver too. All the time they were getting older and a little more broken apart. When he was young he'd thought life would be a process of becoming more certain, but now that he was thirty-three he could only see it as a process of becoming less so. He thought of the careful way his father had moved along the hall, as if even an action as straightforward as walking was now something to think about. Oliver's throat felt thick and painful. 'Do you want these trees, or not?' he said.

Oliver had assumed he would just carry the pots into the garden and leave; it was dark, after all. You couldn't plant trees at this time of night. But his father reappeared from the kitchen with an old spade, dragging two shopping bags containing plastic demijohns filled with water. He was dressed in his waterproof jacket, gloves and a woollen bobble hat. Before her stroke, Oliver's mother had taught herself to knit. She'd started with scarves and made her way through hats and pullovers, ending up with knitted dolls to hold toilet rolls; she'd given all of them away. There was a time when the local charity-shop windows were full of little wool dolls, all sitting on toilet rolls as if they were hatching. But that was by the by.

Oliver's father had fastened a blue plastic bag over each of his shoes and secured them at the ankles with rubber bands.

'Do you want some bags too?' he said. 'I have spares.'

'What for?'

'To protect your shoes.'

Oliver glanced at his sneakers, so battered his toe was beginning to work its way through the canvas, and said he could manage without the plastic bags.

'Shall we head off?' his father said.

'Head off?' repeated Oliver with a strange new sensation of scrambling to keep up with his father. 'Why? Where are we going?'

'To plant the trees, of course. I have my list here and my map.' His father slipped several receipts out of his pocket along with two rumpled pieces of paper. He unfolded them and checked them carefully, then pocketed them again before Oliver could look.

'What list, Dad? What map?'

'My list of where the trees must go.'

'Aren't they going in your back garden?'

'Goodness, no,' said his father, as if this was really so obvious it didn't need to be said.

Oliver checked his watch. It was already seven and he felt worried about Sal. 'Is this going to take long? I kind of need to get back . . .'

His father didn't seem to hear. He passed Oliver the spade and one of the bags of water. He gave a plasticky rustle as he moved with his homemade shoes in that new, careful way towards the porch.

Outside, Oliver opened the passenger door of the van for his father and loaded the bags and the spade into the boot. Maybe his father wanted to deliver the trees to friends? Maybe they were presents? But why, if they were presents, would he need a shovel and plastic bags on his feet? His father had never mentioned friends or presents or indeed going anywhere. Meanwhile, his father had a question of his own. What was that smell? Oliver said it was probably the goat and his father said, 'You drive a goat in a van?' and Oliver said it was a long story. He liked using the same words Binny had used. It was like briefly holding her hand.

How had he got to a place where he had to imagine connections instead of having them?

Oliver drove with his father directing left here, right there, slow on this corner, you might want to get in the left-hand lane, as if Oliver were a complete stranger. Oliver still had no idea where they were heading and his father seemed in no hurry to enlighten him. The old man sat upright, with his seatbelt carefully clipped over his lap, and his list in one hand and his map in the other. The pavements were already jostling with New Year's Eve party-goers, the cheap bars flashing their neon signs. Briefly Oliver scoured the crowd for Sal, asking himself if this was where she had come, wondering who she was meeting. Maybe his father was taking his trees to the crematorium, though Oliver assumed it would be closed. They could just leave them at the gates. No one would steal twenty little trees on New Year's Eve. Oliver could still be home by nine.

And once again, thinking of *home*, Oliver's head tripped and he had to reshuffle the pictures in his mind. *Home* was not Binny's house, blockaded with her parents' old furniture and smelling of so many things it was like a riot in his nose. It was not the small house that smelt of chicken soup where he'd grown up. *Home* was a flat on the fifteenth floor where he was living now with Sal. A flat that had no furniture and one single futon and his guitar under a blanket, because his songs, it turned out, if you heard them over and over again ('*Can you shut the fuck up, Oliver?*') were so crap they were enough to make a woman scream.

Oliver slowed the van as they reached the crematorium, but his father didn't even turn his head. 'I think there might be rain tonight,' was all he said.

'Do you actually know where we're going?'

'Oh yes.'

'Are you going to tell me?'

His father tapped his nose and laughed. 'Confidential information,' he said. Caught in the flashing street lights, his father's old face shone blue and green and yellow as if there were a party going on inside him.

They drove for another fifteen minutes. They were in the sprawling outskirts of the city. The streets widened into bypasses. Rows of semi-detached houses were wrapped like parcels in garlands of lights. Then the bypasses turned to dual carriageways and the houses were replaced with warehouses and retail outlets. Some sites were no more than wasteland, abandoned before building work had finished and surrounded by security fencing and signs that warned DANGER. KEEP OUT. Surely they weren't heading for the motorway?

'Here we go,' said his father. 'You can park anywhere.'

'Here?' Oliver said, braking too fast and indicating as an

afterthought. 'Are you sure?' All that Oliver could see was a road intersection and a roundabout. He parked the van hurriedly.

'Oh yes,' said his father. 'Absolutely certain.'

It was hard dodging traffic. It would have been bad enough if Oliver had been alone, but it was a lot more difficult with an old man, a potted twig, a demijohn of water and a spade. People kept honking horns and making faces as if the two of them were drunk. One driver even slowed to let down his window and asked what the hell they were playing at; Oliver shot out his hand and grabbed his father's arm. And the step up to the grassy roundabout his father had set his sights on was clearly higher than he'd anticipated. His father kept trying to hoist himself up and rocking back again. In the end Oliver almost pitched him. Cars were whipping right past.

'Are you sure this is a good idea?' Oliver said. Actually he shouted. The traffic was loud and he was nervous.

'This is exciting,' shouted his father.

'Illegal is what this is.'

'Do you need a hand getting up?'

'If you put a tree here, Dad, the council will just dig it up.'

'They won't even notice,' said his father.

*

Planting the first tree was far harder than Oliver expected. His hands were sore after ten minutes where the shovel handle bit into his palms, and his shoulders ached. He should have thought to check the blade before they left, because it was so blunt it was like using a wedge of wood, and the ground didn't help. After those ten days of mild weather and winter sunshine it clung together in stony clods. Oliver managed a hole that was six inches deep and about as wide.

'There you go,' he said.

'Is that it?'

'Isn't that enough?'

His father took hold of the spade. He rested his plastic-bag shoe on the lug, the shaft against his leg, and stooped his shoulders. Oliver watched his father's great sweeping movements, letting the spade take its own weight as it cut through the soil. After a little while his father began humming something. He looked right with a shovel, alone in the dark, as though he'd grown solid.

'The thing is,' his father said, 'to lift the tree gently out of the pot. We don't want to disturb the roots, you see.'

Oliver passed him the tree and his father eased it out of the pot like a magician lifting a rabbit out of a hat. He even said, 'Hey presto,' and, despite himself, Oliver laughed. There *was* something slightly magical about the evening.

The Christmas lights in the distance, all that traffic speeding past, no one knowing that Oliver and his father were planting a tree right in the centre of things.

'Lower it into the ground,' said his father.

'Supposing I break it?'

'It's a tree. You can't break it.'

'And how would you know?'

'Look how many of them there are in the world.'

So Oliver rested the tree in the hole while his father slowly lowered himself to his knees and began scooping back the dug-out earth with his bare hands. He filled the cracks and patted the soil firm. Oliver thought of all those summers he'd played alone on the beach, building sand-castles while his father sat beside his mother. He thought of Sal staring with horror at her pregnant belly. And it occurred to him that his father had been frightened of getting it wrong, even with sandcastles. That was why his father rarely went anywhere. That was why he never did anything. Because he had always been so certain that, faced with the challenge of being a father, he could only fail.

Oliver knelt beside his father. He picked up the hard earth and broke it into smaller pieces and pushed it around the tree. The trunk was no wider than his finger.

'I'm going to be a dad,' he said.

His father continued to arrange the earth around the fragile trunk of his tree. Oliver wondered if he'd even heard.

'You're going to be a granddad.'

There was still nothing from his father, only the scratchy scraping of soil. Then, '*Ish, ish, ish.*'

Oliver turned. The old man's face was damp. His mouth was hoisted into a shape that showed his teeth. *Ish, ish, ish.* He was laughing. His father was laughing with happiness, and seeing his father laugh like that, Oliver almost laughed too. It was the first time he had told anyone about the baby since breaking the news to Binny. Sal didn't want to hear a word about it. Oliver continued to pat the soil alongside his father, their hands meeting and moving away again. It suddenly seemed terribly important that they did their best to help the little tree.

'Well, well,' his father said. 'Well, well. Is that with the nice woman?'

'What nice woman?'

'The nice woman with those kids?'

And the happy feeling was gone, as suddenly as it had arrived. Oliver felt a weight plummet through him, like being filled with lead. His shoulders sagged. His head dropped. 'No, Dad. It's not. It's . . . someone else.' He couldn't even speak Sal's name.

Sometimes everything in life seemed right. You had all the things you wanted, all you'd hoped for, only when you looked properly you realized they were all in the wrong context, as if without noticing you'd drifted into the wrong story. Oliver had no idea how he would ever set things straight.

His father opened a water bottle and trickled a steady circle of water around his tree. 'Cheers,' he said, more to the tree than to Oliver. He pulled his list from his pocket and drew a pencil line through the first item.

Oliver and his father went on to plant all twenty trees that night. It took several hours. They drove from the roundabout to the empty car park of a nearby shopping centre, where they dug three holes in a grubby square of grass. Apparently a nice young woman worked on the tills and she'd been telling Oliver's father that she had no garden. They planted one tree in a concrete planter that was sprouting litter and dead dandelions, and two more trees in a neglected flowerbed alongside a bus stop. With his map on his knees, Oliver's father directed them to bare plots of mud and scrappy, uncared-for banks. Clearly he had worked it all out. They planted trees alongside benches and waste bins and in two overgrown gardens where the curtains were towels and the front doors were held together with planks of wood.

'A nice Muslim family lives here,' said Oliver's father, whispering as he watered their new tree.

'How do you know them?'

'Oh, I don't,' said Oliver's father. 'I just pass them sometimes. On the bus. I see them playing with their little boys.'

They drove on to plant a tree outside the GP's surgery, because apparently the receptionist was having a hard time with her daughter, and then they dug in another tree near to the new skate ramps.

And at last Oliver asked, 'Why tonight, Dad? Why trees? Why all these people?'

To which his father frowned, as if he had been given a particularly difficult set of sums to work out, and then shrugged his shoulders. 'Why not?' he said.

The last tree they saved, as Oliver had suspected, for a bald patch of earth outside the gates of the crematorium. Oliver cleared away the rubbish that had accumulated there, the bags and tin cans, the broken bottles, whilst his father dug a careful hole. Neither of them spoke any more. It was almost midnight and they were tired. When the tree was settled in the ground, his father poured the remaining water around its base and wiped his eyes. He put a pencil line through the final item on his list.

'You OK?' asked Oliver.

'Would you mind taking me back now?' said his father.

Faraway cheers went up, followed by a distant peal of bells. Fireworks blossomed over their heads like silver flowers.

In the van his father got confused with his seatbelt and kept trying to slot it into the catch and missing and trying again. Oliver had to reach over and do it for him. He noticed for the first time that his father smelt of something that wasn't chicken soup after all, but something sour, medicinal almost.

'You sure you're all right, Dad?'

'I get a little headache, now and then.'

'Nothing serious?'

His father's mouth worked open and shut, like the seatbelt, but nothing came. He placed one hand on each knee and turned to watch the street. Oliver started up the engine and flicked the indicator to pull out. His back was sore and his palms stung with new blisters, but he felt strangely exhilarated. He didn't feel like a son any more and neither did he feel like a father. He wasn't sure what he was, but he had a sense that he liked it.

Already the Christmas decorations and posters were starting to come down. New adverts would soon replace them, for spring clothes and summer holidays. The girl in the red coat – the girl who been displayed everywhere that winter, caught in a shower of snow, the girl whose appearance on billboards and buses and in the advert breaks on television had embodied the spirit of Christmas, despite the fact that in reality there had not been one flake of snow, only ordinary cloud – had become torn and battered in many of the places Oliver passed. He still had no idea what the advert had been for. Maybe it had just been for Christmas itself. People had drawn beards and spectacles on the girl's pretty face and graffiti hats on the woodland animals. They had added slogans of their own. For a moment it seemed strange to Oliver that people went through Christmas like this every year, putting up trees and coloured lights that would only be taken down again, and visiting people they ignored for the rest of the year, and spending money they didn't have, and eating food they'd otherwise avoid. And then he thought, so what? It was only as mad as planting twenty trees. And where was the madness in that, when you thought about it? Life was a thing to celebrate.

As Oliver and his father turned on to the High Street and crawled through the traffic, they passed a group of young women vomiting into the gutter, and men swaying as if the pavement had turned to liquid. A group of Father Christmases posed for selfies outside a pub and further along, a woman cried outside a phone box. 'Poor thing,' said Oliver's father.

When they stopped at the traffic lights next to the Chinese restaurant, he said, 'Look, that man's having dinner with his sons. That's nice.'

Oliver followed his father's gaze to the restaurant window. Sure enough, a man was pulling a cracker with a tall, black-haired boy and they were laughing at the effort. The second boy, much smaller and with a halo of blond hair, looked straight out to the van, caught their eye and waved. Oliver's father lifted his hand and waved back. The traffic lights turned to green.

A little later they slowed and stopped again, this time outside a ladies' boutique, where three people stood with their backs to the street and gazed at the window display of wedding dresses and party frocks. And this time his father said, 'That person in a green dress is a boy.' He turned his head to keep looking as the car moved on.

'It takes all sorts, Dad. Anyway, you can't talk. You're a guerrilla gardener.'

While he drove, Oliver wondered whether things would go back to being as they had always been with his father, talking about the weather and the traffic on the phone every Sunday, or whether they would plant more trees now, perhaps move on to flowers and vegetables. He could not know that within a few months his father would be gone, and that the old house where he had grown up would be sold, and his father's and mother's belongings, the knitted items, the broken things, even his own child-hood possessions, would be thrown out or given away.

And one day, of course, it would be the same with Oliver too, and the house he would soon share again with Binny, the things they would collect over the years – the school reports, the children's shoes and toys, the feeding bottles and muslins for the baby Sal would not want to mother, the paper mobiles Coco would make – one day all those things would be given away or sold. It was the same for everyone. The coming and going. The little things left behind.

Oliver was pulled out of his thoughts by applause. Applause? How could that be? He cast a glance at his father, but he was asleep already, one hand on each knee, neat and not moving. Nobody in the street was even looking at Oliver and the van, let alone clapping. They ran, some of them, with their arms gripped above their heads, whilst others were standing still, looking upwards and laughing. Nevertheless, there it was. The tapping of many hands, as if the world was saying to Oliver, 'Yes, you planted trees on New Year's Eve. You got it right this time. Well done.'

And then he noticed the pips of water on the windscreen, the smudging around the wipers, the splashing on the tarmac and pavements, and realized his mistake. It was rain. Rain on the roof of the van. They hadn't had any for so long he'd almost forgotten the sound. Oliver wound down his window and breathed in the sweet, dusty smell of it. As he turned the van left, right and left again, rain fell on the streets, the people, the trees, the rooftops, the lights, and he watched.

A story only made complete sense when it was over, when you could look back and say, this happened and then that happened and so this is where it ended. Oliver's story was not over, it was still happening, and the night he planted the trees was just a new twist. He could learn from it or ignore it. The choice was his.

Oliver drove, like everyone else, towards another year. Towards whoever and whatever he would meet next.

Rachel Joyce's new novel, *The Music Shop*, is published by Doubleday in 2016.